THE LOST CRUSADER
A Novel About AIDS in Ethiopia

by

Patricia A. Bluemel

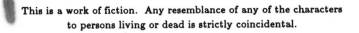

This is a work of fiction. Any resemblance of any of the characters
to persons living or dead is strictly coincidental.

FIRST EDITION

Copyright 1998, by Patricia A. Bluemel
Library of Congress Catalog Card No: 97-90540
ISBN: 1-56002-762-2

UNIVERSITY EDITIONS, Inc.
59 Oak Lane, Spring Valley
Huntington, West Virginia 25704

Cover by Brendon and Brian Fraim

Dedication

In Memory of JB

"The sole purpose of the Scriptures is to inspire
a practice of compassionate action and
the nature of compassionate action is that
we take the trouble to actually get involved
with the person or people concerned."

—Dr. med Juerg Paul Otto Bluemel

ACKNOWLEDGMENTS

My sincere thanks to Lucy Brown, Denise Bardan and
Renate Thevarajah for their support

INTRODUCTION

Deep in the bush of Ethiopia, hundreds of kilometers from Addis Ababa, far from the eager eyes of journalists or critics, the ongoing human dramas of international aid are played out everyday.

For those left behind in the busy centers of western life, little is heard of the daily activities of an NGO, in this case a Church funded organization, unless one is recipient of those accounts usually published by religious organizations for their own interest, that being to promote the ongoing donations which support their cause.

The story found within the confines of *THE LOST CRUSADER* is based in part on a true experience. The book is first a story about Ethiopia, AIDS and then a story about a mission. It seeks to evoke the reader to question what we westerners attempt to export in the form of aid to Africa.

THE LOST CRUSADER does not seek to discredit all Church funded organizations or missionaries. The reader is reminded that the heroine of the book is in fact a missionary. It does however question the art and style of practices in the spectrum of "international aid," primarily Church funded NGO's, which the author finds questionable as we collectively evolve into a global society attempting with more sincerity to provide genuine assistance to our African brothers and sisters so they can solve the innumerable challenges which stand before them.

CHAPTER ONE

It was a Sunday, early afternoon, late in the dry season as the grass-hut village of Aguna lay still, parched in the afternoon heat of an African sun. Except for a swarm of sub Saharan bees, Aguna was immersed in a stupefying silence, uncomfortable at first for any westerner, for Aguna offered no modern diversions, no phone, no TV, no stereo, no shopping malls.

Jack Bronson sat in his favorite armchair in the pleasant coolness of his chica house reading a tattered La Carre paperback, one that weathered the rounds of many readers, an unread book in the outbacks of Ethiopia being a cherished commodity.

The tin roof crackled in the intense heat. "How about a coffee?" his wife asked. Jack smiled and pressed down the page of his spy thriller. The house was seemingly dark, the wood shutters sharply angled, a defense against the glare. In every way it seemed like one of those typical Sundays of late March until a faint indiscernable noise, barely audible, broke the silence.

"What's that?" Catherine asked putting her cup down on the table.

"Beats me," Jack replied as he ambled over to the window, pressing the shutters wide open. A surge of heat swirled into the room as he gazed over the dry mountainous landscape in the direction of the uncomfortable distraction of blasting horns.

"It can't be a wedding at this time of year," Catherine mused.

"No," Jack said now identifying the source. "Come look, there are five pick-ups speeding towards Aguna." For a few minutes Jack studied their progress. They were no doubt headed for the Aguna hospital. "It's probably for me."

Jack walked to his desk, opened the drawer and took out his tobacco tin to prepare his pipe. He was the doctor on call this Sunday. The commotion of the blasting horns broke the deep silence; something was wrong but this did not unsettle the experienced American doctor, whose specialty as a general practitioner was handling emergencies.

He lit his pipe, and casually putting his stethoscope in his pocket, finished his coffee. "Why don't you come up with me?"

"Perhaps later," Catherine smiled as she poured herself another cup of coffee.

"OK," Jack grinned as he walked toward the door.

Outside he was immediately engulfed in the heat. It was not a long walk to the hospital, only five minutes or so, and it was not without enjoyment; there was the magnificent view of the grass hut landscape of rural Ethiopia, the plowed fields, herds of cattle and fields of teff grain.

Jack passed the brick homes occupied by other foreigners, mostly German missionaries and some Scandinavian medical staff. He was deep in thought as he walked. In his mind's eye he was writing a letter to his Lion Club friends, asking them to send a distillation system to Aguna so he could manufacture much needed IV fluid for the hospital and its rural clinics, but the ever increasing noise of the trucks interrupted him. They were climbing the last hill now to the compound.

"They will be here in 10 minutes; I'll prepare one of the examining rooms," he muttered to himself as he rounded the entrance to the mud-built hospital, a view which would make his American counterparts gasp with disbelief. The old building was collapsing, but for Ethiopians the Aguna Hospital was a place of miracles, the major medical facility in the region. Apart from it, there was little option 600 kilometers west of Addis Ababa.

CHAPTER TWO

The blasting horns were now seconds from the entrance to the Aguna Hospital. Jack and his on-duty assistants hurried out to greet the entourage. "What could be the emergency? Breach birth or maybe a needed cranectomy." He flinched, it being the most gruesome of medical situations he had encountered here. Many life-threatening crises were related to the event of child bearing. "But five pick-up trucks would never accompany a woman in need," he determined, for rarely in this society would a woman be given that much consideration or care.

The fact is that the status of women in Ethiopian society is sometimes difficult for a westerner to fully comprehend. A woman is more often considered a possession belonging to the nearest male next of kin, father, brother or husband. Often she is considered of less value than the livestock; the family donkey, for instance, so needed as a source of transportation. And all too often, as Jack had witnessed, when no donkey was available, it was the woman of the family who became the means of transportation, responsible for carrying the heavy jugs of water from the nearest river or the firewood for the family fire.

Suddenly there was the screech of trucks skidding to a halt, dry red dust hurled into the air and anxious faces pushed open the doors as passengers jumped down from the back screaming, "Doktori, Doktori!"

Jack was tugged into the direction of the second truck. A door was flung open exposing a young man drenched in blood lying on the laps of two women.

"Ato Deresu!" Jack shouted not seeing him as the mass of onlookers instantly grew. "Ato Dirba! Get these people away from here, get them in the waiting room. Get Deresu here, I need help in moving this patient!"

There were now crowds of people at the entrance to the hospital. Jack struggled to carefully ease the wounded man on to the tarpaulin stretcher. "Gently, gently," he instructed Deresu, the on-duty health assistant. "Ask what happened to him?"

Deresu asked quick questions in Oromo. "He's been wounded in a political shooting at the market place in Ghimbi."

"Take him into the examining room, Deresu."

7

The crowd of Ethiopians, a mixture of family members, relatives, friends, onlookers and political witnesses pressed behind the stretcher. Jack knew it was the culture that the family could even accompany him into the examining room, but this time he decided to act otherwise.

"Dirba, have everyone stay in the waiting area. No one comes in with us! Let me examine him first and then I will come and tell them the situation."

Dirba, a newly graduated health assistant, responded immediately, gently calming the mass of people who squeezed themselves on to the long wooden benches of the waiting area. This was Dirba's special talent. He had a good way with patients as well as anxious friends and relatives which is why he had gained the attention of Jack Bronson. Dirba was a rare example of compassion in action. Especially in this rural area where it was the cultural practice to be concerned with one's extended family or at most one's tribe. Jack Bronson had thought not once but several times that he might see to a nursing scholarship for the young health assistant. These were the people needed in the medical profession in Ethiopia.

The hospital waiting room was a mud brick room, dark and dreary with an uneven mud floor. On the wall hung a large wooden cross at the base of which were small holes where mice could be seen scurrying back and forth. There was relative silence and some quiet sobs as Jack and his assistant Deresu cut the clothes off the wounded patient.

Jack felt the man's pulse, took out his stethoscope and listened.

"I know him. He is the son of the most famous merchant in Ghimbi," Deresu explained. "He is even a graduate of the University in Addis Ababa." From this information Dr. Jack surmised that if the young Oromo died, if the family or tribe would lose such an outstanding member, it could fuel a political crisis.

"Get a blood sample to the lab Deresu, find a relative who can give blood! He is in bad shape! Get a runner to call Vandenbos! Tell him he has emergency surgery to do. Get someone to run after the OR staff. I'll get some IV."

"But . . . doctor . . .?" Deresu's voice faltered.

"I don't care what Vandenbos says . . . now we use an IV!" Jack commanded catching his cool, for if anything raised his temperature it was the idea that Vandenbos, the missionary surgeon and long-time director of the Aguna Hospital, would not use IV during operations and would forbid anyone the use of them. The rumor among Ethiopians was that the surgeon kept them in the event the foreign staff, the missionaries in particular, required it.

"Unbelievable!" Jack had so often thought. "Why not

manufacture your own IV fluid here in Aguna giving work to the people and make IV fluid available to every patient, black, white, foreigner, native or missionary."

Just then Jack's attention focused on two young men racing out of the entrance of the hospital; one running up the steep hill into the village of Aguna to call the OR staff, the other down to the Aguna compound to Dr. Vandenbos's house to call him for surgery.

CHAPTER THREE

The waiting room was full, Ethiopian style. As is the common cultural practice, eight Ethiopians crammed together where one would normally find at most three or four westerners. It was one of the significant cultural challenges for Jack Bronson. Either he was surrounded with students, even as he walked from room to room within the small hospital corridors or as he drove the pick-up which according to Ethiopians was not full unless four or possibly five people were squeezed in the front seat, unless twenty or so were riding on the back.

When Jack Bronson now entered the waiting room, there was an immediate hush. For a second he studied the anxious faces. It was more than a severely wounded boy's welfare at stake, this was also a matter of tribal politics. A fatal outcome could provoke civil disturbance. Here in the outbacks, there was no police force to call for assistance. There was only the military who would take any measures needed to squelch an upheaval.

"Ladies and Gentlemen," Jack began, as Ato Deresu translated into Oromo, "your friend Abebe has been badly wounded. He has lost much blood. He has been shot in the stomach," Jack continued, speaking slowly and very simply so he could not be misunderstood. "We are asking the appropriate relatives now to donate blood." As he was about to continue, one of the tired runner's flew into the entrance of the waiting room waving his hand, trying to get the attention of Ato Deresu. Jack did not stop but concluded his message.

"As soon as Dr. Vandenbos comes, he will operate and try to stop the bleeding. Meanwhile, we will try to do all we can. Thank you."

Ato Deresu rushed over to the runner and turned to Dr. Bronson with a blank exasperated look.

"What is the problem?" asked Jack.

"Dr. Vandenbos is in his Sunday prayer session, he will not come now!"

Jack stared at Deresu in disbelief. "Sunday prayer session! What the hell does that mean? There is surgery to be done!"

Jack looked briefly at his watch. What did that mean? Would Helmut Vandenbos come or not? Minutes seemed like hours. Jack leaned his head out of the entrance of the hospital door, along the path which sizzled in the afternoon heat. Helmut was nowhere in sight.

Jack Bronson, JB for short, as he was more commonly called, partly because it saved time, more comically because JB was the name of his favorite whiskey, returned to check the patient in the examination room. A few OR nurses had now arrived and were attending to the patient. JB stepped into the next room, grabbed a scrap of paper and wrote, "Helmut this is urgent! Young man shot in stomach, surgery required now. I have set up the OR. JB." He gave the note to the runner.

The minutes dragged by. He checked the OR room and decided to move the patient inside. More time could not be lost. As he did so the exhausted runner returned with a note in his hand.

"Helmut will come when the prayer session is over." The note was signed by Vandenbos's wife, Ingrid.

"Is this the real world?" JB's mind began to spin with incredulity. He did not know Helmut well, but realized after first impressions that the man was certainly cast of a different stuff then he. An image of JB's father flashed into his mind. The memory of a special day so many years ago, when JB's father had once asked him what he wanted to be when he grew up. JB answered directly, "like you, a doctor."

"Are you so sure? It is a tough job," answered his father, "and we Bronsons, the entire family of whom I will remind you are doctors, are not in the profession of medicine like a lot of others, we are not doctors to impress society, or to satisfy our bank accounts but rather to be of total service to patients," he lectured strictly. "However, if you think you are really interested in this profession, let us first see if you have all that it takes. I will arrange for you to be under the supervision of one of my best nurses, Sister Tante. I will instruct her that you are to be her assistant, that you are to do the most menial tasks, like empty bed pans and bathe patients, do you understand. If you impress Sister Tante with your work and you still want to study medicine, I'll have no problem seeing you through medical school."

Because of this early experience whereby to first satisfy the demands of his father, JB first had to become a fully certified nurse, he not only came to endorse his father's approach to medicine but was a faithful example of his father's medical philosophy.

For JB, the patient always came first. His life and medical career revolved around the patient. He knew other doctors had different priorities; for some it was money, some the status the career of medicine brought, but JB could not conceive being in the outbacks of Ethiopia where a medical emergency was at hand . . . and a prayer session took priority!

JB knew he had to act. He would not ask . . . but inform Helmut that he would operate on the boy. This, he thought, would cause Helmut to react. Either Helmut was attempting to teach JB that a prayer session took priority over an emergency or could it possibly be that Helmut was afraid to do emergency surgery of this sort. Of course, it was a risk. Now there was only a 50/50 chance for the boy to live, but at least we must give the patient the chance he deserves, after all that is one reason why they have medical staff in Aguna.

He grabbed another sheet of paper. "Helmut, if you are not here in five minutes I have no other choice than to perform the surgery myself. I cannot sit here and watch someone die while you are in a prayer session. JB."

Again the runner was off down the hot pathway along the compound.

CHAPTER FOUR

JB turned his attention to his patient, checking the boy's pulse and his heart. He was significantly weaker. He would not wait for Helmut any longer.

The OR was a very small room with open windows and a small sink in the corner from which no water flowed. On the edge of the sink was a tin can. It would be filled with water for the surgeon to wash his hands in preparation for surgery. An old tattered towel hung next to the sink on the wall. JB had washed his hands and was turning to the towel when Dr. Helmut Vandenbos abruptly walked in the OR.

The bean thin, white-haired German missionary doctor did not speak, he did not even greet the staff or JB. He looked at the patient with disinterest. "Gun shot wound in the stomach?" There was a moment or two of pause. "Is he a member of our Church?" Helmut Vandenbos questioned.

JB did not answer. His thoughts focused on the patient until he noticed a curious deep and long cut on Helmut's right hand. The old hunch backed surgeon who had himself promoted on the international circuits as the "Great White Doctor Of Ethiopia" began to examine the patient's abdomen, his hands now covered in blood.

"You'd better use gloves Helmut, that looks like a nasty cut you have," cautioned JB.

"I don't use gloves and I don't use IVs like you either," Helmut snapped. "A waste out here!"

"Haven't you ever heard of AIDS?" JB warned. "This young man is from Addis. He has been around. With any patient, you should take some precaution. Be careful, Helmut. It doesn't help if you get sick."

"There's no AIDS out here," growled Helmut under his breath.

JB could not believe what he was hearing. Was Helmut just upset having been called out of his prayer meeting or did he really think that there was no AIDS.

"And I'll ask you not to mention that sickness again if you please. This is a mission hospital."

"What does that have to do with AIDS, Helmut?"

"You can go, Dr. Bronson. I'll take over."

"I'll be glad to do the surgery, if you'd rather not. You haven't forgotten Helmut that I too am a surgeon but I am trying to live according to the mission regulations which requires your permission for any surgery. You are aware I hope that it is time to act, the patient is getting weaker. Christianity is not just the act of praying. It is more importantly doing!"

Helmut glared at JB as he turned to walk out into the waiting room to address the crowd. They looked at him anxiously. He smiled and tried to reassure them. "Dr. Vandenbos is now here and he will do what he can for your young man."

But no sooner had JB said this did Helmut burst out of the OR angrily wiping his hands of blood on a worn towel.

"I'm not going to do surgery, for your information, Dr. Bronson!" announced Helmut, "sometimes decisions are made by God himself and we are not to interfere with His decision."

"And just how are you sure this is His decision!" JB asked.

Many Ethiopians understood the English. "Let Doktori Jack help please," one woman shouted, "let him operate, we want to take the risk, it may save him."

"I make the decisions! No surgery will be done!" Helmut bellowed, his eyes twitching madly as he returned back into the OR.

JB's face turned ashen. Catherine who had meanwhile tucked herself in an obscure corner of the room off the waiting room, witnessed the unfolding drama. Her heart sank as she looked at her husband. Never, never had she seen his face so pale, so expressionless. Never did JB look so defeated.

The waiting room was stone silent. "Sit with us," said the Ethiopians. Jack Bronson took a seat on one of the wooden benches, his head bent way down, his hands clasped. Catherine came to sit beside him, the Ethiopians who were speechless graciously providing some space to sit. There was nothing more to say and the Ethiopians knew it. They sat for more than an hour when a teary-eyed Ato Deresu appeared outside the OR. "Our Abebe, our friend, has just died." There was only two or three seconds of quiet before the Ethiopians unleashed their mournful cries and wails.

JB got up and slowly left the hospital and headed down the compound. He was mortified, ashamed for the mission medical staff, embarrassed by the events of the afternoon and deeply regretting the treatment of the dead young man and the lack of care and sensitivity shown to all involved. It was as if this event had violated all his medical ethics, his approach to the practice of medicine. "I would have taken the chance and done the surgery!" he said strongly under his breath as he looked up at the sky. "There was a good chance for the young man. I know it! Why didn't Helmut act! Why didn't he do surgery! At least let me

14

try? Was there something behind his non-action? Could it be a kind of revenge? Helmut after all had lost his own son in a motorcycle crash. The rumor was Helmut Vandenbos never talked about it, the accident being just a matter of God's will and all that. But what if Helmut was just afraid to take the risk, losing the patient, losing his reputation as the 'Great White Doctor'? It couldn't possibly be that the boy was an outsider, a non-Church member, that he was Muslim . . . or?" JB wondered.

At first, Catherine began to follow her husband until she stopped, realizing it was perhaps best for JB to have time alone. Her deep dark eyes welled with emotion. "Such insensitivity!" she thought as she watched Helmut, trying to read his mind from the grim expression of his face. Helmut's eyes momentarily caught Catherine's. She turned away just to find herself face to face with two inquisitive German missionaries merely curious as to what all the Sunday commotion could be about.

Catherine felt a wave of agitation which she could not contain. Never before did she recall being so angry, so full of emotion, so passionate. "What is all the excitement about?" inquired Willie, one of the pastors, with a smile.

"You have missed a grand example of missionary kindness, of missionary tolerance and compassionate action, Reverend Willie," Catherine spurted out.

"Oh, how sad," responded the pastor.

"Quite frankly, Reverend Willie, I have come to the very sad conclusion that this hospital is quite possibly a sham!" her long hair slowly unfurling. "It flaunts itself to the outside world as a haven for the poor and needy where in fact it is a haven for self righteous fundamentalists who appear not to have a clue about compassion. I wonder, Reverend Willie, if I were to write about this, if the outside world would believe me? What do you think?"

The two missionaries looked expressionless which only caused Catherine's anger to mount. The two were void of any reaction, without feeling or visible concern. So a young Ethiopian had died. It did not really have an impact on their lives. However a day or so later, they take the opportunity to visit Mrs. Bronson counseling her that perhaps she was suffering from an early onset of menopause, for no Christian in their right mind would ever criticize God's work, the great work being done at Aguna Hospital.

As a psychologist, Catherine knew the Sunday event had sparked a deep emotion within her. It had triggered a remarkably strong reaction which caused her to dwell on the matter. "It is the hypocrisy of it all. It is the way they tell the donors in the west of all their great Christian activities, and the reality of how they really act in the seclusion of the bush of Ethiopia. All their actions are condoned because they are in the name of God," she

15

thought. For more than once she had heard the mission staff excuse what Catherine considered their rather rude and insensitive behavior by the fact "Christians were not perfect and God always forgives us."

It was in fact . . . not the first time Catherine and Jack had the feeling that all was not well in Aguna. "But why here," Catherine mused, "why am I confronted with such a situation in the most unlikely of places, the bush of Ethiopia and in the company of missionaries who I expected to be the most compassionate of people?" And of greater concern to Catherine was how she could continue to live under these circumstances. The Bronsons had a three-year contract. "Somehow I have to find a way to cope for JB's sake," she thought.

CHAPTER FIVE

Long whispers of blue smoke filtered through the grass huts on the hillsides around Aguna. It was early morning. The villagers had started their fires. Outside their tukuls, women pounded beans for their morning coffee. As the sun crested the mountains, the cool moisture of the valley evaporated, causing steam to float up magically, unveiling the landscape. The loud chatter of the monkeys and baboons gave way to the clucking of hens, the haw of donkeys and mooing of cows. Catherine was up early as usual, dressed in a long cotton dress, her hair neatly done in a French twist. It was her favorite part of the day. Catherine felt that there was a certain specialness of mornings in rural Ethiopia, like being on another planet, a kind of exotic drama, the experience should never be missed.

"Strange," Catherine would think to herself as she gazed across the morning hillside, at the different lifestyles we share on this one small planet and such differences could be experienced just with the small task of preparing coffee.

Diribe, the Bronsons' household girl, would boil water for her morning coffee over an open fire in her tukul. She drinks it with salt for lack of sugar, while Catherine used an old Scandinavian wood burning stove. She and Jack would drink their coffee with sugar just because they are lucky enough to afford the exorbitant price. Often as Catherine was making her morning coffee, she could not help to think about these discrepancies and would laugh to think that Lucy, Catherine's friend way back home in Fort Lauderdale, would be sure to use her microwave and her artificial sweetener.

As breakfast time passed, JB would leave to make rounds at the hospital passing Diribe and her cousin, Techilu, as they came to work at the house. There was always plenty to do. In Aguna there were no machines. All work was done by hand with Ethiopian help, the washing of clothes, the cutting of grass, the chopping of wood.

By ten o'clock in the morning, the wood burning stove was fuming like a dragon, eucalyptus smoke seeping out of every crevice. It was a time for ironing. The old fashioned blocks of iron were simply placed on a tin sheet on the stove to heat.

Ironing was crucial, not so much a matter of fashion but a matter of health, a protection against the dreaded mango fly which would deposit its eggs into the damp laundry. Once the towel, bed sheet, or shirt made contact with human skin, the eggs would embed themselves deep within the flesh and incubate causing huge welts, infection and high temperature. The only relief was the horrendous ritual of removing them with knife or needle.

After lunch, there was no unnecessary movement. Aguna was hot and bush silent, the foreign staff finding relief in short naps and the Ethiopians resorting to the cool shade beneath the trees.

In the late afternoon, however, when the heat abated, Catherine would take the opportunity to talk into the village. It seemed always to be a psychologically uncomfortable excursion, but how could it be otherwise. Inevitably, she would catch herself peering unobtrusively inside the huts, scrutinizing the inner decor, the scarcity of acquisitions, the thin mat beds, the one or two wood stools, perhaps a crude table, but always to Catherine's horror . . . a coffin. This served a variety of purposes she was later to learn, a place to sit and when not employed for its ultimate purpose, a place of temporary storage.

As Catherine observed the locals, they always intently studied her, what she wore, how she moved. Balloon-bellied children stared as if watching a thrilling movie. Barefoot women hunched over with loads of firewood or jugs of water stopped and stared and then would smile.

The thousands of years of isolation had left rural Ethiopia as a primal theater, a reminder of humanity's very beginnings and yet nearing the 21st century, Catherine feared that the outbacks of Ethiopia had been hopelessly left behind and that they would never manage to enter the hi-tech age of the outside world and thereby be forever forgotten, assigned to hopeless poverty and sickness.

And then, just as Catherine was lost in such contemplation, there was a faint sound way above Aguna. Her stomach cramped, she felt slightly light-headed. Instantly, she knew it was 4:30. It was the Addis Ababa-Khartoum flight. An eerie reminder of civilization, what she had left behind, that other life of glossy magazines, the latest from the cinema, perhaps a cool French Chablis. For Catherine, the unaware travelers evoked a disturbing sensation, one of acute homesickness. "Just for an hour, I'd like to be up there, just for an hour a chance to be away from this hopeless poverty, just for an hour to be away from this compassionless Aguna and the likes of Helmut Vandenbos and his partisans."

For there was no real escape from the confines of Aguna, no other town to visit, no other friends to see, and the Bronsons were to discover they were not to be well accepted among the mission community on the small compound of Aguna.

CHAPTER SIX

Outside the deteriorated chica medical facility, a line of subdued patients and their relatives waited in almost absolute quiet for their turn at the reception window. Amidst the ailing was a barefoot woman in obvious pain who clung to an unfinished wood railing which made order out of the waiting mass of people. She was covered in an earth-stained shawl, her dress torn and ragged.

Workitu was very pregnant. She had been in and out of labor since the early hours of the morning. Her sister and husband, having urged her to go to the mission hospital had accompanied her on the three-hour journey. Now they were standing in the channeled line waiting patiently.

At a snail's pace, the people moved closer, nearer the window where a health worker was busy pulling cards and more importantly collecting the newly mandated fee of six birr.

As Workitu's turn finally came and she reached the awaited window, her discomfort became pronounced. She sucked in her breath in an effort to control herself. Her sister, noticing her distress, cut in front of her and spoke on her behalf, explaining to the health worker that she had complicated labor pains.

The health worker asked for her name and inquired if she had been a prior patient. Her sister answered, "no." The clerk shoved a card and pencil into the sister's hand directing her to fill it out. But the woman could only hand the items back because, like so many others, she could neither read nor write.

The health worker huffed his disapproval, retrieved the pencil and card and promptly demanded the fee of six birr.

"Six birr?" questioned the sister. "We don't have six birr. We thought it was only two birr."

"Then, I am sorry, the fee is now six birr," retorted the health worker with no emotion, already focusing his attention on the next line.

Workitu hearing the conversation winced in pain, sinking onto her knees like an airless balloon. The health worker regarded her with disdain but from the corner of an examination room, Gette, an Ethiopian midwife, was watching.

The sight of Workitu caused a flood of memories for Gette,

memories of that awful night she had finally arrived at the Aguna Hospital, after a miserable four-hour walk in the rain, tired and hungry and in pain and also without money. Her husband had been killed in the ongoing civil war leaving her destitute. Tears now came to her eyes. For had it not been for the intervention of Sister Elizabeth, a kind Norwegian nurse, who miraculously had been on duty that night, Gette would have never had the C-section she desperately needed, the operation which saved not only her life but that of her beloved daughter. Now Gette was a mid-wife herself, thanks to the efforts of Sister Elizabeth.

Gette wiped the tears from her eyes. She knew it was God urging her on to take some action. But how? For the last year, Dr. Vandenbos had imposed a new policy at Aguna. No staff member had the authority to admit a patient who could not pay the fee, no matter what the circumstances without his permission. And the admittance fee was no longer the two birr that Gette could not pay but six birr, a sum few rural Ethiopians could afford to pay. The problem was that six birr was the equivalent of one US dollar, a sum most foreigners would seem affordable for anyone in the world to pay for entrance to a hospital. But that fact remained, for the majority of rural Ethiopians, their yearly income was about 250 birr making a six-birr admittance charge for medical attention out of the question for once inside the hospital were all the additional charges for care. A traditional healer surely cost less and could be paid with chickens, eggs and other payments in kind.

What could she do in the situation? She feared Dr. Vandenbos would not accept the woman. Who could she find to help? Sister Elizabeth was on leave in Norway. Perhaps, she thought, the new Doctor Bronson might help. She had heard he was quite sympathetic.

CHAPTER SEVEN

The tea break was every morning at 11 AM at Pastor Ulbrig's house, which in Catherine's opinion, was a most depressing setting, unimaginative and somehow typifying the lack of style which seemed now peculiar to the mission community. Here around an extended table covered with a worn green plastic cloth, decked with fifteen brown plastic mugs in between miscellaneous papers, piles of religious magazines, heaps of dirty clothes, scattered toys and views of unmade beds, the teas were served.

There was little question but that the tea break had to be held at the Ulbrig house. This family required an extra long table and many chairs. There were six children, a big family, characteristic Catherine observed of missionaries committed to long periods of stay in the rural regions. The tea and coffee break was organized by Edith, Pastor Ulbrig's wife. It was a shared venture, the coffee and tea being provided by the various households of the compound, each being assigned a specific day. Tuesday was the day assigned to the Bronsons and so Diribe and Techilu busied themselves in the morning preparing the three pots of coffee and the two pots of tea which they then hustled up to the Ulbrig house along with a bowl of sugar, spoons, a pitcher of milk and the corsii. The corsii was the ritual tea break snack, an Ethiopian dish. In essence it is a huge pancake made out of teff, the native grain, rolled up, cut in three-inch segments and covered with a mixture of spices.

In reality, however, the Bronsons were well aware that the Aguna sponsored two tea breaks, one for the Ethiopian staff held in an open hut and the other for the foreign staff. But Ulbrig, the missionary, would explain it otherwise. "Well, one tea break is for upper staff and the other one is for the lower staff."

It was no secret now to the Bronsons that the real reason was that the foreigners wanted to avoid the musty odor that the Ethiopian staff could generate and "well there is always that chance of picking up fleas" the mission staff would not hesitate to point out.

Tea break appeared to be a forum for Dr. Vandenbos, to dominate the conversation with his wife Ingrid who found joy in

21

revealing the mission news from home. Over time, Catherine and Jack Bronson found themselves more often seated at the other end of the table, that reserved for the more quiet members of the staff, those who would not volunteer for words of religious testimony, spontaneous prayers, or accounts of miraculous events.

On this particular Tuesday during the tea break, there was a knock at the Ulbrig's door. "Is Doctor Bronson there?" asked Gette nervously and shyly.

"He is having his tea," answered Ingrid with a firm tone, "is it so important at this very minute?"

"Well," Gette began diffidently, her voice quivering.

"Just what is the problem?" chimed in Helmut Vandenbos, curious as to why Jack Bronson would be summoned instead of himself.

"What can I do for you?" JB replied now being aware of Gette at the door and wanting to spare her any further embarrassment.

Gette tugged at JB's shirt sleeve so as to avoid their being overheard. "There is this poor woman, Doctor, could you please, please help?" she whispered.

"Well of course I can. Just what is the problem?"

"Sh, sh . . .," Gette signaled. "It would be best if the others did not know."

JB and Gette left the room and started to walk up to the hospital, Jack greatly relieved to have an excuse to cut the tea break ordeal short. "A woman, she have delivery problem, is lie outside the hospital on the ground," Gette began in her broken English.

"Why in heavens is she outside?" JB inquired, now picking up his pace.

"Well, she does not have enough money to get admittance and I just thought you maybe able to help her, you see I have no authority," Gette tried to explain but could not find the English to go further.

Outside, in the waiting area, Jack Bronson found Workitu lying with her relatives around her under a nearby tree. "Is this your patient, Gette?"

"Oh yes, doctor," Gette smiled with relief.

"Let us get her inside into a bed immediately."

"But, the fee, doctor!"

"If she is too poor, the fee comes out of our special fund for poor patients, Gette. She does not need to pay."

"Oh, Doctor Bronson, I glad you are here. You help us much," said Gette pathetically pleased that the desperate woman now would receive help, that her intervention was successful.

CHAPTER EIGHT

Later that morning, long after the tea break, JB was monitoring several health assistant students as they attempted to learn how to diagnose patients when Gette came racing into the examination room. "Oh, Doctor Jack," she whimpered, "I don't know if I should tell you. I don't want . . . trouble."

"Tell me what?"

"Well," she whispered, "it's that pregnant lady, the one you said should have C-section . . . soon as possible."

"Yes, Gette, calm down, I have scheduled her in twenty minutes for the OR."

"Well . . . Doctor Bronson, she . . . she . . . told to leave."

"What, what do you mean Gette?" JB answered now with his full attention. "She has to have a C-section. How can she leave?"

JB tried to piece Gette's cryptic message together. Gette again tugged at JB's sleeve pulling him over to the window. "There, do you see . . . they leaving, doctor!"

JB watched with astonishment as the threesome labored up the hill outside the hospital. "What is going on?" he whispered to himself. He turned to Gette, "is she so afraid of the operation? I thought they accepted the idea without hesitation."

"They could pay no money, so they . . . told to go, doctor."

JB didn't ask any further questions. "Come with me Gette, I need you to translate," he ordered. They both walked briskly outside after Workitu and her relatives, their white uniforms instantly becoming dusted from the red powdered soil. "Ask where are they going! Ask them if they are still willing to have the operation! Explain that I will pay for it myself. They have no reason to worry about the cost."

"Essa demtu?" (Where are you going?), asked Gette in Oromo. The husband explained, "There is no poor fund anymore at Aguna and we do not have the six birr to pay for admittance." But tears came to the relatives eyes as soon as Gette explained that it was all settled, that Dr. Bronson would take care of the payment.

"Now tell them we will go back all together and I will take care of her immediately."

As they slowly made their way back to the hospital, Gette

23

thought about the situation. Perhaps she should enlighten Dr. Bronson further. "You see Doctor, I . . . get in trouble for helping this lady. We . . . people like Gette, not to admit anyone who no pay."

"But who says that?" asked JB. "What about the fund for the poor?"

"It is rule and we were told again just last week at meeting. We were told that the hospital must now make money."

"Who decided that? I have not heard of any such nonsense, Gette. Are you sure? How can this be called a mission hospital if it does not accept the poor. In fact, one of the premises it can operate out here is that it accepts those who cannot pay. This much I do know for sure."

"What a hopeless lot, incompetent from the word . . . go," JB thought. "They seem only to care about preaching the gospel but no interest in practicing it."

"Who has told you all this at the meeting, Gette? Who told you . . . not Dr. Vandenbos?"

"Sh, ssh," Gette whispered. By this time they were entering the waiting room. "I bring Workitu into the OR but there will be trouble later on with Dr. Vandenbos. You will see, Doctor."

"Gette, please, please do not worry about Dr. Vandenbos. I will take full responsibility for Workitu and her relatives."

"If a hint of what Gette said was true," JB thought, "if in fact Helmut Vandenbos dismissed a woman in need because she could not pay, that would be the last straw. I could not support this hospital or Vandenbos anymore. In fact, I would dedicate the rest of my time in Ethiopia exposing the inhumanness of this so-called Great White Doctor Of Ethiopia and his clan of so-called do-gooders."

JB washed his hands for the surgery, continuing to think . . . "Was Helmut Vandenbos actually mad or was he just a power-hungry ego-maniac who had been left too long in the bush of Ethiopia unsupervised?" In any event, the old missionary doctor had lost JB's respect. Vandenbos and his lot were not what he had expected to find out in the bush of Ethiopia, not what he expected at all where so many patients were desperate for help.

CHAPTER NINE

It was the following Monday morning, about 9:30, when Pastor Ulbrig knocked on the door of the Bronson house.

"Ah, good morning," said Catherine, taken with surprise, "please do come in Pastor Ulbrig. How about a cup of coffee?"

"No, no," replied the thin aloof pastor whose primary occupation was sitting before his books all day, revising a translation of the Bible into the Oromo language.

"Well, then do sit down. How nice of you to make a visit, Pastor Ulbrig. I do not see you too often. Your work consumes so much of your time I suppose," Catherine found herself saying, wondering all the time just what would bring the cold religious bookworm to her door.

"Ah, well, it . . . it . . . it is a . . . ah . . . about your husband," the pastor stuttered.

"So sorry, Pastor Ulbrig, but JB is not here at the moment. He has gone to deliver some medicine to a nearby clinic."

"The mi . . . mission community has a . . . asked me to come here to talk to you about him," finished the pastor.

"The mission community, or do you mean Dr. Vandenbos, Pastor Ulbrig?" questioned Catherine, slowly realizing that there was a big agenda at hand and that the pious Pastor Ulbrig, a disciple of Helmut Vandenbos, had been sent as an emissary. "Well, never mind, they are one and the same, aren't they?"

"It . . . it . . . has to do with his be . . . behavior as a Christian," the pastor continued.

"What behavior?" inquired Catherine.

"His . . . his smoking a pipe for instance."

"But that he does only at home," Catherine explained emphatically.

"People know about it, it . . . it isn't part of mission behavior."

"So, it is not the Ethiopians who complain but just the mission?"

"Well . . . we . . . we want to set a pure example as did Christ," explained the pastor whose thin scarce blonde hair danced upon his head. "And there are other offenses."

"Like?" asked Catherine.

"Well . . . well, it . . . it is his admitting this pregnant woman, Workitu, for instance, without requesting permission from Helmut. Then he . . . he even drove her home in one of our pick-ups. We . . . we . . . we just don't do that here. If one does that, it . . . it makes the rest of us look bad for not doing it," the pastor said. "We therefore have . . . have decided that before Dr. Bronson uses any of . . . of the pick-ups for the hospital work, he must fill out a form, this form," and the pastor pulled out a few sheets of paper from a folder.

"But, Pastor Ulbrig," Catherine interjected, "JB pays personally for any mileage on the pick-ups when he transports patients and these patients are often too weak to walk the miles to their homes. Don't you feel if one doctor here feels that is how he wishes to spend his free time, it is acceptable, especially by a mission?"

"This form must now be used," repeated the pastor.

"And as for admitting Workitu, does my husband have no authority to admit a patient to the hospital? He paid for the hospital fee even though there is supposedly a poor fund donated by people we know in the U.S."

"O . . . Obedience is a Christian virtue which your husband does not display, Mrs. Bronson," said the pastor getting up from the chair. "It is time for me go go now. I will see you at the tea break Mrs. Bronson, won't we?"

He got up and walked out the door. Catherine remained sitting, tears coming to her eyes. She glanced at the calendar on the wall. "How will I make it two and a half more years in this place?"

Just a few minutes later, the door flung open. It was JB. "Time for the tea break, isn't it?" he grinned.

"No, not ever again!" burst out Catherine crying.

"Oh, goodness! Whatever has happened?" Jack asked kneeling down before her.

Catherine described the events of the morning, the visit of Pastor Ulbrig.

"Catherine," Jack said softly, "we are not here for these missionaries. We did not come to Ethiopia to serve the likes of Pastor Ulbrig or Helmut Vandenbos or any of these missionaries. We came to Ethiopia to help and serve the Ethiopians. Forget these people, it is just a power game and only a handful of them have any interest in helping the Ethiopians. The rest are interested only in when they can leave and tell their big missionary stories back home to get applause. If we help the Ethiopians our actions can't be wrong."

"I will not go to this tea break anymore," Catherine said looking at Jack. "Even if it makes us look even less Christian, if that is possible," Catherine added.

"We will start to have our tea breaks at home free from the

26

hammers of God," JB chuckled, "at least here I can have a short pipe. Actually, I'm glad not to go. Tea at home is the best news I could think of."

Catherine began to smile. "Good, I was hoping you'd agree."

"Catherine," JB chuckled, "you should know by now I don't do things to impress the hierarchy here or the US or anywhere. You really should understand this!"

"But you know now it may get mean. We are beginning a strategy of withdrawal from this community. They will use this as a further example of our disobedience," Catherine responded.

"Catherine, don't be afraid to do what you believe in."

"I don't condone their interpretations of Christian practice. Prayer, for example, takes priority before actively saving someone's life, increasing the hospital fees, even when they know the people can't possibly afford it, just to impress donors. I can't pretend anymore, JB. I can't! How do I survive two and a half more years. Tell me that!"

"First, obviously," JB chuckled as Diribe brought in their coffee, "you are not going to the tea break anymore. It is your first step to opposing what is going on here. Secondly, have you ever considered studying the problem out here, putting it under a microscope so to speak. Why not think of taking this obvious negative situation we are in and before giving up, before leaving, why not try to make something positive out of it," JB offered.

"But how?" Catherine questioned.

"Become curious why you are here. Find out what your purpose is to be in this situation. Ask yourself what you are to learn from it. Study this situation, then find a way to share what you have learned with others so what you have learned is not lost," explained JB looking at Catherine with eyebrows raised as he lit his pipe. "This is nice . . . tea break at home. Why didn't we do this much sooner?"

"Catherine," JB continued, "I have been thinking about this for some time. You love studying, you want to finish the doctorate you started in psychology, you love writing, why not combine all these interests now. Write a paper for the Journal of Theocentric Psychology, entitle it "Life in the Company of the Great White Doctor of Ethiopia," JB chuckled.

Catherine began to laugh. "I think tea break at home could become dangerous with such ideas. But I love it. Thank you, JB, you just turned my world around."

CHAPTER TEN

It is not certain where the word "farengie" was coined. Some suggest that it is a mutant derivation of "frenchie." In any case, "farengie" or its shortened form "farenge" had come to designate any white face in Ethiopia, French or not. During the course of time, a white face had become symbolic of money, scholarships abroad as well as other related support.

In Aguna, the "farengies" were by profession missionaries, the greater majority theologians, the remainder, medical staff, who under the strict guidance of Dr. Helmut Vandenbos promoted a very conservative form of Lutheranism, for the benefit of their Ethiopian sisters and brothers and, which further extended in some cases to those "farengies" who they considered to be of dubious Christian belief. The Bronsons were now included as part of their mission.

The Aguna compound Bible study was held every Wednesday night at 7 PM at the Vandenbos home. There was no question who would lead the Bible Study. It was never a theologian as one might expect but Dr. Helmut Vandenbos, considered the most pious of the missionaries, an example for all the staff to follow. It is of interest to mention that Helmut Vandenbos's influences exceeded the Bible study and included also being the Director of the Aguna Hospital, the Chairman of the Aguna Compound Committee, the Executive Chairman of the Aguna Mission Church and the Director of the Aguna Mission School and leader of all spiritual activities to include the weekly Bible session.

"It all fit together," Catherine thought recalling the first time she had ever seen Vandenbos. It had been in the compound generator room to which he had the only key. That was the first time she had ever seen him standing before the 'switch' as it was called which if Helmut flipped on, permitted the compound to enjoy an hour or so of electricity. "All the authority at Aguna lay in one person's hands," Catherine pondered. "It all exclusively belonged to Helmut Vandenbos."

It began promptly at 7 PM, the weekly Bible study that is. With somber expressions, the missionaries would file in with Bibles and notebooks and pens. Dr. Vandenbos would always stand as he began the two-hour session, opening his heavily underscored Bible, worn from the years and years of use during his long missionary service. Tonight's Bible Study was on the topic of obedience.

"The dictionary defines obedience as 'to carry out orders.' The Bible however, says," began Dr. Vandenbos, "I am reading Romans 6:16 . . .," he paused, eyeing his favorite Swedish nurse. There was a shuffle of turning pages. The missionaries had opened their Bibles, flipping pages. "Obedience is a matter of righteousness."

Catherine opened her notebook, first to give the impression of her astute attention, secondly to just jot down thoughts. "Such dark companions of theology," she found herself scribbling. She knew that the Bible Study was directed to the Bronsons, especially JB. The message was clear . . . JB was to obey Helmut.

The long, drawn out lecture continued with a solemn missionary grimness. So unlike the atmosphere that Catherine had experienced within the traditional Ethiopian Orthodox Church. The Bronsons had secretly attended the rich and festive celebrations of the Orthodox. Catherine recalled once on the festive day called 'Timkat,' in the west known as Epiphany, where the Ethiopians would parade through the streets displaying the celestial spheres, the ornately embroidered parasols in the procession. The sacred tabot, the symbol of the Ark of the Covenant, wrapped and obscured from view in beautiful brocades was carried by elaborately gowned priests while the excited crowds would erupt into exultation, shouting and singing, stomping the pavement as tambourines, cymbals and sistras played. Women and men pirouetted and swayed, jerking their shoulders and bobbing their heads as they danced as David had once in the presence of the Ark.

The unique history of this Orthodox Church, its colorful celebrations, had greatly inspired Catherine. It was as if Christianity held an element of enchantment that the missionaries had lost.

"JB, did you ever consider why we were never told anything about the history of the Orthodox Church at the mission preparation course before coming to Ethiopia," Catherine would often like to discuss. "Why do you think that was, they just forgot perhaps?"

As the weeks went by mysterious big parcels arrived in Aguna for Catherine. The entire mission compound was curious what the contents could possibly be. And even more of a surprise, it appeared that Catherine Bronson had vanished from the community altogether.

She was busy, very busy indeed, reading and taking notes. Her bookshelves were suddenly adorned with such texts: *A History of the Ethiopian Orthodox Church*, *A Psychology of Mission Sciences*, *A History of Christianity*, *The Church and*

Mission as a Psychodrama.

"Today I had the most remarkable interview for my paper with Ato Teferi," Catherine began to explain to JB as he sat to light his pipe at their now traditional private tea break.

"Ah, and what did you learn?" smiled JB, snuggling back into his chair to enjoy a morning coffee.

"I asked him the list of questions that I prepared and in answer to the question, 'What has Lutheranism brought to your people that the Orthodox Church has not?' he answered, 'The missionaries tell us that they have the short-cut to heaven, the one and true gospel and this cannot be found in the Orthodox Church.' Isn't that an amazing answer?"

"The short-cut to heaven," JB chuckled. "Do they actually say that, literally?"

"Yes, Teferi says that is how they respond to any comparison made with the Evangelical Lutherans and the Orthodox Church," Catherine explained.

"Very interesting," JB said thinking, "it really reflects their behavior, doesn't it."

"How can they be so pompous? Have I missed something out here? I don't feel that I am experiencing a short cut but a great big detour, a stone wall in my Christian experience," Catherine said laughingly. "But to claim that someone has the short-cut to heaven . . . that is the last straw!"

CHAPTER ELEVEN

At first there was a quiet tension, controlled and mostly unspoken, the mission compound of Aguna aware of increasing difficulties in the Gulf, and the probability of conflict escalating into a war. The short-wave radios portrayed Saddham Hussein as an evil, ruthless tyrant who must be dealt with. Each night with compulsive concern, the Aguna community turned to the BBC in silent hope of peace; the Gulf was not that far away.

Yet as their cares were drawn to the plight of Kuwait, peace was slipping away in Ethiopia as well. There was an unsettling air, an uneasiness, potentially explosive, which was unfurling across the entire country.

The main road to Addis Ababa was now closed due to military activity. JB delayed his trips to the surrounding clinics, though at such a time he knew the medical facilities would be more dependent than ever on his resupplies of medicine and his assistance in treating the casualties of the ever increasing military conflicts. But the missionaries were uneasy, and did not want their pick-ups to leave the compound.

At night the Bronsons could hear gunfire in the far distance, and one morning the unspoken tension amplified into considerable apprehension with the news that a UN truck had been destroyed by a mine, leaving three people dead.

Though the Oromo people with whom the Bronsons lived comprised at least 50% of Ethiopia's population, historically, they had led a nomadic life. Due to their long pastoral background, the Oromos were considered a gentle people, a patient and passive folk which historians consider the reason why they have been oppressed throughout their history by the more agressive Amhara tribe. The message of the Oromo people, their story of virtual constant domination, remains largely unknown to the outside world. And even in this more opportune time, the escalating civil war in Ethiopia, once again the focus of the world's media did not lie in Ethiopia or Africa but rather directed towards the trouble brewing in the Middle East and the Gulf and the demise of the Soviet Union.

It had all started by some frightening news. A German development worker, driving in the direction of Addis Ababa with his wife and son, were fired at, not once but some twenty-five times. Their bullet-ridden pick-up truck had limped on to the nearest hospital. Mr. Althaus, a specialist in agricultural services from Dembidolo was badly hurt, his legs shattered and splintered. His wife and son miraculously survived the assault.

The event sent sharp ripples of fear throughout the international community. Was the OLF (the Oromo Liberation Front) targeting foreigners to get international press, finally seizing an opportunity to be heard by the outside world?

The foreign families with children shuddered to think that the white missionary could become a target of Ethiopia's conflict as well. Heretofore the missionaries felt immune to civil conflict and unrest but now the mission compound had become full of uncertainty. Was it possible that they could become vulnerable? This fact seemed to influence their often quoted commitment: "that no matter what the situation . . . we keep teaching the gospel." Overnight it appeared to be revised: "No matter what . . . but for my complete safety . . . we keep teaching the gospel."

CHAPTER TWELVE

In October of 1989, a Soviet advisor was dispatched to Ethiopia. His mission was to visit the communist dictator Mengistu Hailie Mariam. The advisor's message was short and simple: "You have to solve your own internal problems, (Menguistu), the Soviet Union cannot support your expensive activities any longer, our future is not certain."

Menguistu was then 49 years old and had ruled Ethiopia for fourteen years. He was a man with only eight years of formal education and liked to fashion himself after his idol, Fidel Castro of Cuba. Menguistu gained his power in Ethiopia by killing King Hailie Salassie, ending the direct line of King Solomon. He had the body of the former king buried under his office in the palace. It had been a bloody coup and Menguistu had been one of the few survivors.

Over time, Menguistu acquired the title "the other butcher of Africa." His managerial style included personally executing those who failed to please him. The media reported that he made a trip to the town of Nekemte for the sole purpose of killing 50 of his senior officers. Nekemte was not far from Aguna.

However, Menguistu had now become desperate. How would he continue to fund his on-going civil war, how would he remain in control? Eritrea was posing a serious threat, it wanted to be independent. Like a rat caught in a corner, Menguistu re-established ties with Israel with devious intent, hoping that Israel would influence Washington, make fast amends for 15 years of socialism, and thereby acquire financial support for his military schemes.

Menguistu did not stop there. He condemned Saddham Hussein and announced his allegiance to the U.S. campaign in the Gulf. Apparently President Bush had even called him. Menguistu assumed financial support was forthcoming.

While Menguistu was busy fund-raising for his cause, the Oromos realized their opportunity as well. They, like their Eritrean cousins, could also fight for their independence.

The OLF, the Oromo Liberation Front, began their assaults, their main target, the government forces. Mines were laid randomly along the main roads, the first casualty being a UN truck carrying supplies to the Sudan Border.

Menguistu deployed more troops towards the west to fight the OLF. Aguna therefore became more and more tense. Truck loads of wounded soldiers came daily to the hospital. The missionaries were on edge as embassies issued alerts for all foreigners.

CHAPTER THIRTEEN

By the time JB had reached the radio room, it was crowded with excited people, ruffled by the announcement of a further standby (radio contact) in half an hour. The political situation had seriously deteriorated. Everyone was jittery, nervous with speculation.

"95 do you read?" shouted Helmut Vandenbos.

"Yes, 79 go ahead," was the weak and static reply. It was Addis Ababa. "Who is reading, over?"

"Dr. Vandenbos, over."

"Here is Dr. Mann, Helmut. The following messages have been issued by the American, Norwegian, German and Finnish Embassies . . ."

They had all issued an alert, general warnings regarding the crisis at hand. Some made suggestions that it was time to consider evacuating Ethiopia.

"95 do you read?" Vandenbos repeated the messages making sure they were accurately received.

"79, this is Mann speaking. Now for the co-workers of the mission, the following travel advisory . . ." then he faded out. Further communication was impossible. The radio was being mysteriously jammed.

As Helmut turned the radio off, the compound mobilized into action. Like a flock of birds suddenly taking into the air without defined reason or direction, there was a restless movement and anxiety. The missionaries were talking, exchanging points of view, debating their future action.

And then Helmut Vandenbos took charge, as usual, ordering everyone for a meeting at his house. There was much excitement. Helmut tried to get the group to be quiet without success. Then, finally a discussion began, dividing the mission community. JB and Catherine stood silently in the back observing the developing drama.

Theological lines were being drawn, imaginary of course but nonetheless more impenetrable than real. There were those who would comply with the recommendations of their respective embassy and others who would defy any such order.

"My orders come from God himself, only He can tell me and

my family to leave," spouted Pastor Ulbrig.

"But you have the well-being of eight children to think about," replied one co-worker.

JB made a slight yawn. He stood near the window and gazed out on the magnificent view, into the exquisite valley, the tired sun making preparations for its sleep, slipping gently behind the acacias and sinking into the earth. He thought about the people of Ethiopia, all the special Ethiopians he knew. He was concerned about their future. He knew now the missionaries would be of no help to them. In the chaos they only thought about themselves.

Inside the living room, the discussion and rediscussion, the hashing and rehashing of plans continued with no resolution.

"I'm leaving to go have a pipe. Come with me," JB whispered to Catherine.

"Good idea," she replied.

Outside the living room was the instant relief they both sought. It was a lovely sunset, a beautiful evening.

"It is no doubt best for you to pack a suitcase or two; I would want you to leave at the first opportunity," JB advised.

CHAPTER FOURTEEN

A young woman placed a gnawed plastic tumbler on the table. She tipped a tin kettle filling the mug to the brim with the most inconceivable concoction. JB eyed the mixture, scrutinizing the peculiar inclusions which lifted to its surface.

"Those things are spices," assured Ato Fufa pointing to the dirt like specks as they swirled on the crest of the mud brown ferment.

The drink was simply "farsoo," a native Ethiopian beer, the homemade beverage popular throughout the countryside. JB chuckled softly as he surveyed the tumbler once again. There was no fizz, no frothy head, no carbonation, just this thickish brown brew dotted with mysterious floating specks. But now the focus of twelve black Ethiopian eyes rested upon him, waiting in patient anticipation as he lifted the untried portion to his lips.

JB studied his audience as he managed his first swallow, for he was a well-traveled man, having been almost everywhere in the world and he was experienced in the art of handling strange food and drink. His life's adventures had bred an enormous self confidence and now at his age when gray begins to manifest, he found himself thoroughly enjoying such circumstances being absolutely sure of their outcome. Now JB gave a big smile and as he put down the tumbler the Ethiopians broke out in a laughter of acceptance.

JB was the only white face among the six men sitting inside the chica house in Talla. They had radioed Aguna last evening asking for a doctor to come immediately. Helmut Vandenbos said he didn't care if Jack went to Talla, "just don't take any of the mission cars. You can walk, or how about a donkey," the missionary surgeon had laughed sarcastically.

"It is 45 kilometers away, Helmut," JB had said. "How about I take the old blue Susuki, the one no farengie drives because it is too dilapidated."

"Take it, but you won't make your destination, I assure you," was Helmut's advice.

The old Susuki stuttered and gasped its way to Talla. But it did make the journey and four hours later JB found himself on the only upholstered chair in Ato Kumsa's house in Talla, being treated as a guest of honor. Talla had radioed Aguna Hospital before asking help. This was the first time someone had come. They were simply amazed.

In the center was a raw wood table upon which the young woman placed a giant serving plate full of oversized "budenna," pancakes made of teff grain.

The men drew themselves around the colossal dish looking like esteemed academicians, their left hand cupping their right elbow, the right arm held stick straight suspended in the air. They had just finished the ritual of washing of hands and now the right hand was reserved in its more or less antiseptic state for eating the noon day meal. In a ghost-like fashion the woman reappeared, this time with a simmering pot. Without eliciting the slightest acknowledgment, she gently nudged her way to the budenna plate and ladeled hefty spoonsful on the teff pancakes. It was a simple "wot" made from local beans steeped in an assortment of native spices and wot butter.

The steam of the hot food curled its way into the air arousing their tongues and spurring their stomachs. But their craving had to be momentarily postponed. It was time to pray. The men nodded towards one man in a wordless deference. He was to say the grace:

"Yaa waaqayoo abbaakeenna" (Oh God our Father)
(The Ethiopian heads drooped in unison.)
"Irbaata kana nuuf eebbisi maqaa Yesusiin Ammeen." (Bless this food in the name of Jesus, Amen.)

Ato Kumsa, the senior health assistant at the Talla Clinic, was the host. The guests waited for the necessary cue from Kumsa:
"Jed'aakaa innaanna!" (Let us eat!)
Upon those words the one white and six black right hands made an impatient dart at the budenna tearing off small portions which like a sponge soaked up the spicy wot. Their fingers worked madly, forming, molding and squeezing the mixture into mouth-sized balls.

At first it was quiet, for the men were hungry. And of course JB knew that despite the urgency of any medical crisis, it was the culture that first they would share a meal and only after that would the Ethiopians begin to discuss their problem.

CHAPTER FIFTEEN

"Doctor, we see you have boxes inside and on top of your car," Ato Kumsa smiled as he paused from eating.

"Well, I tried to take as many medical supplies for you as I could. It is a small little four wheel, not much room for transporting supplies. But it was the only transportation. Now because of all the civil unrest, the mission won't allow any of their vehicles off the compound."

"We know and we cannot thank you enough for coming, Dr. Bronson, and for the medicine," the men expressed in unison.

Talla was just one of the many small "out-clinics," found in the surrounding area of Aguna Hospital and still within one day's reach by four-wheel drive. The purpose of an out-clinic was to provide basic medical treatment for Ethiopians in the immediate area. Usually such a clinic was managed by a trained health assistant such as Ato Kumsa or, when a clinic was really lucky, by a trained nurse. The Aguna Hospital was to be of support to the out-clinic providing emergency transportation to Aguna if necessary, medical supplies and a supervising doctor.

JB had revitalized the out-clinic supervision program which seemed to have been forgotten, leaving the small clinics badly neglected. Therefore, when any out-clinic would radio for help. Jack Bronson felt it a duty to respond no matter what the situation or difficulty to any request. He had demonstrated his commitment to his supervision program by coming to Talla.

"I could only fit two sacks of milk powder and one of grain on the top," JB explained. "Lucky it is the dry season or I would have sunk into a mud hole."

The men all laughed. They ate at a slower pace now, their appetites satisfied. Again their eyes turned to the same man to give the final words of thanks:

"Yaa waaqayoo, maaddii, kana laatee waan nu qufssiteef si galateeffanna maqaa goftaa Yesusiin. Ammeen." (Oh God, we praise you in the name of Jesus that you gave us this food and satisfied us. Amen.)

39

A young boy was sent in with a plastic bowl of water and a pitcher. He held a thin bar of soap and a towel. Each of the men washed their hands, and the young woman refilled their mugs with the farsoo.

"We really need your help," Ato Kumsa announced to JB. It was now polite to discuss the business at hand. "There is a meningitis epidemic underway. Over half of the admitted patients are infected and in serious condition. By nightfall I expect half of them to be dead."

It was viral meningitis, a disease affecting the brain tissues. JB had seen his share of cases. Relatives would carry the patients for miles on stretchers to the Aguna Hospital explaining, "it seemed only like he had the flu yesterday, Doctor, but now he is so weak, such a high temperature and stiff neck."

The patients were naturally admitted and treated as well as possible. But for many they were diagnosed too late and there was little hope. Many would die. The people were generally malnourished to begin with, their bodies offering little resistance to the attack. Now it was the height of the dry season, the conditions were ripe enough to awaken the deadly virus.

"The people are frightened. So many die. We don't know the exact number because most of them never make it to the clinic. They die quietly at home," Ato Tolassa, a junior health assistant explained.

"These two gentlemen here, Ato Zelalem and Ato Jonas, are from the United Nations," explained Ato Kumsa. "Since we did not get any response from our letter to Dr. Vandenbos for medicine, we wrote to the United Nations and they have brought us vaccinations, syringes, and needles. With two trucks and a team of seven health assistants we could vaccinate and save 50,000 people."

"Did you say you wrote Dr. Vandenbos about this?" JB inquired with curiosity.

"Yes, we sent a runner with a letter to him a few weeks ago," Ato Kumsa replied.

"You never got any response?"

"Well, just to the effect that he couldn't help you at this time."

JB didn't ask any further questions. "Let us go to your radio. Let us ask for a standby with Vandenbos. Meanwhile I will go and look at your patients in the clinic. I could stay here and we could begin the vaccination program and Aguna can send two more trucks and staff down this afternoon."

"You are the help we need, Dr. Bronson," Kumsa said with a smile.

"You are the kind of foreign doctor we need out here."

CHAPTER SIXTEEN

They huddled in a small mud shack next to the clinic.
"Doctor, sit here, sit on this sack," Ato Kumsa offered. The
Ethiopians were always kind to their guests and even in the most
rural of areas attempted to provide the most comfort they could.
The small room was full of sacks of corn that the Talla Clinic
had harvested. The military was on the air sending a host of
uninteresting messages, the reception was garbled.

"79, do you read, this is 55, over," said Ato Kumsa. The
radio sat on a wooden board on a small ledge in the corner.

"This is 79, go ahead 55," said Dr. Vandenbos.

"Here Doctor, you talk to Vandenbos. I am sure it would be
easier," Ato Kumsa said handing JB the microphone.

"Helmut, it is JB. There is a medical emergency here in
Talla. There is a meningitis outbreak. The UN has provided all
the serum, they just need our help to distribute it, two trucks
and about six or seven staff. Can you send them this afternoon. I
will stay here to begin the work, over."

"55, the answer is simply no. I told Talla Clinic we cannot
support their problem. We have no trucks available at this
time . . . over," said Helmut.

"79, what do you mean we have no cars. Send the pick-ups
and some staff, that is all that is required. Ato Kumsa has
managed to get everything else on their own. At least we can
help them vaccinate the population. They have a real problem,
Helmut, over!" pleaded JB.

"You know our policy. Due to civil unrest no trucks go off
the compound, over," said Helmut now shouting.

"My God Helmut, this is not Germany! This is an
emergency. We are the only ones in the area who can give
immediate support. We are supposed to be helping the people out
here, Helmut! You can spare one truck to help 50,000 people, the
other one keep on the compound for the 23 farengies if need be.
But at least send one truck. For heaven's sake! Over," shouted JB
with disbelief.

"The answer is no! Over and out!" Those were the last words
of Helmut Vandenbos.

Ato Kumsa let the radio go static before turning it off. They all sat still, JB holding his head in his hands.

"Dr. Bronson, don't take it too hard," offered Kumsa smiling. "This is the way it is here. We are used to this! We are not surprised, not surprised at all!"

"I am so very sorry, Ato Kumsa. I am embarrassed just being associated with this Vandenbos," JB's voice barely audible, his head still bent over. "This is why foreigners come here I thought, to help you with these kinds of problems. I would never have imagined anything like this goes on in mission communities. No one would believe me at home. No one! Not anyone!"

"Let's go to my house for coffee. It will make us all feel better," Ato Kumsa said placing his arm around JB.

The men sat silent once inside the chica house. There was nothing more to say or do they thought. JB, however, was recovering from the disappointment. He was making a plan. He would not be defeated by Vandenbos, not when needy people required urgent help.

"This is what we can do," JB began as Ato Kumsa and the men leaned over to listen. "I will stay with you for the next three days. At least we have this old Susuki. If you UN chaps can stay to help us that is at least two more assistants. We could send runners to the villages. Have the people meet us at one location. We can set up a couple of tables and just vaccinate the entire day as many people as we can. It will be tiring but no-less effective."

"Oh . . . Dr. Bronson, what a plan," Ato Kumsa said, the men all in agreement, "and it will be a great help."

"Luckily," JB said with a chuckle, looking out the window towards the sky, "luckily I brought extra canisters of gasoline. At first I thought that was silly and I was going to leave them behind."

"Sometimes God works in mysterious ways," answered Kumsa. "Your plan is the Will of God, Dr. Bronson."

"Then, let's not sit here, let's get busy. Can you send as many runners as necessary to the villages and tell them that we will start vaccination tomorrow at 9 AM wherever you designate."

Ato Kumsa gave each man their assignments and the activity began.

"Ato Kumsa, can you arrange a standby with my wife Catherine? I had better let her know I am not coming home for a few days."

CHAPTER SEVENTEEN

"79, do you read, over," JB said.

"55, I am reading. This is Catherine. How are you JB?"

"I'm fine, but I won't be coming home for a few days. There's a medical problem here. Over," explained JB.

"Do you need help or something? Over." Catherine inquired.

"It's a long story. In short, Aguna won't send help. Therefore I'm staying. Vandenbos will no doubt be angry. Things could get tense because I've decided to stay. I just want to warn you. Expect the worst. Catherine, please pack everything up, everything possible," JB said. There was a deluge of static on the radio. "I will explain later, over."

"What is wrong? Are you in danger? Is the military there, over?" Catherine inquired.

"No, everything is OK. It has to do with Helmut. I can't explain now on the radio. But I can't continue at Aguna. I think it is best you go to the States until the unrest is over. Please do what I say. Pack! I want to leave Aguna as soon as I get back, over."

"Sister Annemarie left a message for you this morning, JB. She wants to know if you could come and see her at Dabo Gatcho. What should I say, over?"

"Pass a message to her! Have a stand by with her early in the morning when no one else is around. Tell her I'll come and work with her to the end of my contract if she wants. Perhaps you can give her some information on the radio and she'll understand what I'm thinking. I hope you do, over."

"JB, some missionaries are coming up towards the radio room now. Perhaps it is best we sign off. I better stop now. I'll have a standby with you tomorrow at 6 AM, love you, over and out."

Catherine turned off the radio. Two missionaries were walking towards the radio room and she did not want them to overhear any part of JB's conversation. But how do I explain why I am sitting here, her mind raced. As they came toward the room, Catherine had an idea. She turned on the radio and tried to reach "36" Sister Annemarie and arrange an early morning standby. Perhaps this would avert any suspicion that she had

43

radio contact with JB.

"Hello," said Sister Uta, her eyes big with curiosity. "I have never seen you at the radio before. Who are you trying to talk to?"

"Oh, I am just trying to get a standby with Dabo Gatcho," Catherine answered, her insides began to shake. Her mind however, burst with a sudden comprehension. So this was Vandenbos's plan after all to frustrate JB until he quits his assignment in Aguna. And I as JB's wife, I make a good target. If I finally get crazy here in Aguna, then JB would have to leave, he'd have to take his wife out. Why didn't I see this more clearly before. Catherine took a deep breath.

"Dabo Gatcho?" asked the Edith. "Whatever do you want with them?"

Catherine had to be quick so as to avoid too many questions and a long explanation. "Oh, nothing special, just trying to reach Sister Annemarie, but I can do that later. Please ladies, you take over," as Catherine pushed the chair back. "Have a nice afternoon," Catherine said handing Edith the microphone and left the radio room as quickly and politely as possible. She was fast, but well-paced, not wanting to be the focus of unnecessary attention.

As she walked down the long pathway to the house she tried to put the pieces of JB's message together. It seemed to gel all of a sudden. JB wanted to leave Aguna. He must have had another encounter with Helmut.

Catherine felt a moment of immense relief. Her eyes took in the magnificent African sunset. At least this could be the beginning of peace leaving Aguna and its tyrant Helmut and the "flat shoe brigade of female missionaries" whose sole purpose it appeared was to make life unbearable for her. *They will not succeed!* Catherine said to herself, her arm slicing the air. Never!

I'll gladly go home to the States for awhile, she thought as tears flooded her eyes, just to be out of here and away from this nightmare. JB would stay, perhaps he would go to Dabo Gatcho and help Sister Annemarie. Anyhow, until JB came back, the doors must be kept closed and no one should know that she was packing up all the things she could.

CHAPTER EIGHTEEN

"Diribe, keep these shutters closed! Do not tell anyone that I am packing suitcases," Catherine said as she noticed the young girl's face turn sad with tears. It was understandable, if the foreigners left, the local people lost jobs, there was no help, little employment.

"Don't worry! I have a great secret to tell you. Promise not to tell?" Diribe shook her head, her eyes still lowered. "I think Dr. Bronson will be going to Dabo Gatcho and will work with Sister Annemarie. So, he will always be near you. I will go away for awhile. When things are better I will come back, and in the meanwhile, we will leave you and Techilu enough money, OK?" Diribe began to smile. She was so grateful. The Bronsons had been the best thing that had happened to her in her life. "But now you must help me get these suitcases packed."

It took Catherine three days to sort out things. What would she leave behind? What were the most important things to take? Her now thick notebook and journal, her draft dissertation on the 'Theocentric Psychology of Aguna,' a discourse probing the emotional deficits of Aguna which were responsible for the lack of compassion and empathy in the work, was of course the most important possession Catherine now had. Its contents amazingly consumed a good three quarters of one of her two permitted suitcases, leaving little room for anything else. Just as she had finished, the door opened.

"Hi," JB said. "Looks like you've been busy."

"JB! I'm so glad you're back!" Catherine said hugging him. "Gosh, you are stinky and look at this beard," she laughed.

"Is there hot water on the stove! I need a shower quick!"

The Bronsons' shower consisted of an inverted jerry can which hung from the ceiling in the bathroom. The hot water from the wood stove would be poured in the jerry can and that served as the shower.

"First, have a coffee! You must tell me what happened."

Just as JB finished the details of his adventure, there was a loud knock on the door and in burst Helmut Vandenbos. Catherine stood up, caught off guard. "Do come in Dr. Vandenbos."

"Just how do you explain your absence for the past three days," shouted Vandenbos directing his focus on JB who remained sitting with his coffee cup in hand.

"How about a cup of coffee?" JB offered with a slight smile.

"I asked you how do you explain your absence?"

"Easily explained, Vandenbos, as in my radio message to you. I was out helping the people who needed help," JB darted back. "Finally I was able to do something worthwhile out here. We vaccinated 30,000 people in and around Talla. Oh, and Helmut, your little old Susuki performed really well."

"You ask my permission before you do that again. I am in charge," snapped Helmut, raising his arthritic finger, his face turning a kind of crimson.

"No need," JB explained walking across the room to get his pipe. "I am leaving Aguna. It is what you have wanted, Helmut. You should be very pleased." JB opened his tobacco tin, stuffed his pipe slowly and before lighting it turned to Helmut and said, "There is a gross lack of compassion here despite all your Bible studies and church services, Vandenbos. I do not see the practice of Christianity! I can't work with you any longer. I am going where I can help the people without your constant interference." JB paused to light his pipe, smoke curled into the air. I will go to Dabo Gatcho in the next few days to work with Sister Annemarie. I know she is interested in helping the people."

"You cannot just leave and go where you want! This would have to be approved by me, approved by the Synod Medical Committee and the President of the Church in Addis Ababa as well. And how about your supporting organization in the States?"

"It has all been done. I stopped by the headquarters in Bodjii yesterday. It is all approved, the President was contacted and gave his approval. My organization is in full agreement and the Synod Medical Committee as well."

"Impossible! I am the chairman of the Synod Medical Committee. I have to be there," screamed Helmut pacing back and forth across the living room, his eyes blazing with anger.

"Not in an emergency session," JB explained, drawing on his pipe, observing Helmut's erratic gestures, his long white coat waving behind him. "Please, Helmut, sit down."

"What do you mean, emergency session?" Helmut continued, still standing, his eyes twitching rapidly.

"Well, due to the civil unrest and your letter to the Synod that no mission car is allowed off the compound, the Vice Chairman is authorized to—by agreement—to take your place. He did. Everything is approved. You cannot change it."

Helmut's eyes glared in anger. "What reason did you give them that would make them vote in your favor?"

"I simply told them the truth, Helmut, that I did not sell my medical practice in the U.S. and come all the way to the bush of

Ethiopia to serve the whims of missionaries who appear to have not an ounce of concern or compassion for their work but rather I came to Ethiopia to help the people in need. That is all Helmut. They were convinced in a flash," JB smiled as he relit his pipe. "Of course, I had a discussion with the medical staff about the AIDS pandemic as well and told them that they need to set up a program as fast as possible. They were very open to it. They do not deny that AIDS is a raging problem, Helmut."

"You will pay for this Bronson!"

"I have already paid for it by wasting my time here, Helmut."

Vandenbos turned repeating, "You will pay for this dearly," slamming the door behind him.

CHAPTER NINETEEN

"A bush hopper arrives tomorrow at 9 AM," explained JB as he returned from the radio room. "It is the only plane that will risk it out here. They are all afraid of the civil unrest. It will bring mail and milk powder and can take ten people out. Only eight are signed up," JB remarked shaking his head. "The 'holies' like Ulbrig have decided to stay here because God has not spoken to him yet and given orders for him to go with his family. So there is plenty of room for you to go."

"Your face looks brighter," Catherine said.

JB paused glancing out of the window to the valley below. "Ah, I am glad that you can get out, can go to Addis and home for awhile; you need a break from this nightmare, I know. And I think working with Sister Annemarie will be what I need. She has a heart. Oh, by the way I just had a standby with her. She said to keep the words 'white dove' in mind."

"What does she mean by white dove?" Catherine asked.

"Not sure, just keep it in mind," JB replied shrugging his shoulders.

The Bronsons were up early the next morning. Huddled together on their porch steps, they drank a coffee. "It is a funny feeling," Catherine began, "when will I see you again?"

JB put his arms around Catherine. The sun was rising over the acacias. "If it were not for the white people here, Aguna would be one of the most beautiful places I have ever been. But I need more than a view. I want to make some difference with the rest of my life. I feel like I have been given so much. At 52, it is time to give something back, but in Aguna there is no chance to do so. I think with Annemarie I can do what I came to Africa for. At least I want to have the chance to try. I know it is a lot to ask you."

"I understand, I just want to know how long do you think we will be separated?"

"I can't be sure, but as soon as it is OK in Addis, I will contact you."

"OK, JB," Catherine whispered, kissing him.

"Now it's time to go up to the meadow. We have to raise the flag or the hopper won't ever find us."

48

The suitcases were loaded on the back of the pick-up. Catherine hugged Dirbe and Techilu. "If you need anything and it is safe, all you have to do is go to Dr. Bronson and Sister Annemarie. I will see you soon." Diribe lowered her head as tears ran down her face. Techilu tried to control his emotion. No words could express the emotion of events.

There was a light breeze on the meadow. Nine passengers waited for the small mission aircraft. A small flag waved and in the far distance a hum of an engine could be heard.

Suddenly, it could be seen. Everyone took a deep breath, hoping that the OLF rebels would not interfere in its arrival. "They have been advised that we are expecting a small plane this morning at 9," assured JB. "Everything should be OK." Catherine's stomach began to churn. She'd be leaving JB, leaving him behind now in a very uncertain situation. It is what he wants, she thought. It is what he needs to do and I need to go.

The plane now circled the meadow, swooping over the ground as the pilot studied the white-stone-lined landing strip and wind direction. Its small engines roared louder than any Airbus and the mere suspense of its arrival in Aguna seemed more awesome than being at JFK in New York. The wheels touched the grass whipping a flurry of dust into the air. The plane hopped its way bouncing heavily until it came to a thundering halt.

The pilot hopped out, the suitcases and passengers were quickly loaded aboard; and before Catherine knew it, she was waving to JB out of the window and the aircraft raced down the bumpy meadow and lifted into the air.

It is all over, Catherine thought, her eyes flooding with tears as she looked at Aguna from the increased altitude. It looked so small, so lost in the vastness of the countryside. What a place, Catherine mused, what a place of pain. Her story of Aguna was now over, at least for the present. Would anyone ever believe it, understand it?, she wondered?

But for now . . . she decided to anticipate bookstores, caesar salads, friends, relatives and ice cream.

CHAPTER TWENTY

There was a scurry of activity at the radio room, people shouting, anxious faces, strained looks as JB arrived. With Catherine safely gone, he was beginning to anticipate his trip to Dabo Gatcho.

"Doktori, doktori, the Burbur bridge has been blown up by government forces," shouted Ato Deresu. JB picked up his pace, his face full of concern, just how would he get to Dabo Gatcho now if there was no bridge.

"Are you sure, Deresu?"

"Yes, Doctor, we just heard! How can you get your things and medicine to Dabo Gatcho now?"

"Get me Bodjii on the radio now. Have them send a pick-up!"

It did not take long for JB to come up with a plan. The head office in Bodjii would send a pick-up and transport him, his luggage and the supplies to Burbur after which they would have to use rope and pullies to transport the materials across the river.

"36, do you read," said JB sitting at the radio room table.

"Sister Annemarie reading, 79, go ahead."

"I plan to leave tomorrow morning at 6 AM. We plan to be at the river at 11 AM. Can you arrange a truck or donkeys on the other side for supplies. Suppose you know the situation, over?"

"No problem, will arrange. We are aware of the situation. Any further message?"

"No 36. See you tomorrow. 79 over and out."

"All the best. 36 out."

"Oh Dr. Bronson. This not good . . . that you leave us," said Ato Deresu as JB closed the radio room door.

"There is enough medical staff here, Deresu. You won't miss me," said Jack putting his arm around his favorite health assistant.

"Doctor, you know what we mean when we say it is not good that you leave us. We mean that there is no one else who cares so well for the patients and the people as you. Why are you so very different than Dr. Helmut? You laugh with us, eat with us and you even drink with us."

"Perhaps things will be better when I leave, Deresu. You never know."

"But we never knew a difference before, Dr. Bronson. Now we have all seen a different way of being, a new way of caring, that Aguna could be different. It will never be the same for us again.

"Oh, Doctor, a runner came from Talla this morning with this."

JB opened the dirtied envelope. "Dear Doctor. We can't thank you enough for your help those days you were with us. Please, the people here thank you kindly." JB refolded the letter knowing that despite Aguna, missionaries and the likes of Helmut Vandenbos, he loved the Ethiopians. He now had a second chance, a possibility to really be of utmost help.

"You see you're needed here. No one would have stayed to help those people in Talla. You are a good example for us, Doctor," continued Deresu.

"Then start your own health assistant association. Meet together and talk together. Get the head office to come and listen to you. It would be good if you all finally decided what you think you want and need to improve your health care here."

"OK, Doctor. I will start a discussion here. If we ask for you back here in Aguna, will you come?"

JB chuckled. "Well, let's see how far you get, Deresu. And you know Dabo Gatcho has lots of potatoes. Here in Aguna there are none and I love potatoes." The two laughed.

"You will see Doctor. This will happen. Already, there is a letter to Bodjii from the health assistants asking that they keep you here."

"Meanwhile, Deresu, help me pack the medicine for Dabo Gatcho. I want to take as much as I can."

"You have to be careful driving down to the river. If the military sees you, they may rob the medicines."

"We have asked for two government soldiers to accompany us as well as some soldiers from the OLF, it should work out."

"Doctor, you think of everything!" Deresu laughed.

CHAPTER TWENTY-ONE

The next morning the overloaded pick-up quietly crept its way off the Aguna compound under a big African moon which still hung big and fat in the sky. JB was happily behind the wheel. Finally, he was leaving Aguna. Alongside, in the passenger seat, sat Dr. Dawit, an Ethiopian doctor, a good friend and support from Bodjii.

"I'm glad to accompany you, Dr. Bronson. I feel very safe especially when you wear your red hat," said Dr. Dawit with a big grin.

"Why is that, Dawit?" JB smiled.

"Because everyone in western Wollega knows that red hat, the good guys as well as the bad guys," Dawit explained.

"You think so or hope so?" JB chuckled.

"Everyone knows out here, the red hat means the good doctor. The word is out," Dawit continued.

Dawit would ride with JB to the meeting point at the Burbur Bridge then drive the pick-up back to Bodjii. As they drove by the entrance to the Aguna hospital and left the compound, a feeling of great relief swept over JB. "It's all over! No more nightmares in Aguna," he thought.

As the pick-up moaned its way up the steep hill into the village, a second pick-up fell in line. It was full of soldiers who would provide security throughout the journey.

"This Hi-Lux is really loaded," said Dr. Dawit with a grin. "Hope we don't have too many flat tires."

"That is why I called you to come with me, Dawit," JB laughed. "I need someone to change them."

As they cleared the village, the wide expanse of the beautiful Ethiopian countryside unfolded before them. JB increased speed. The two truck convoy sped along the gravel road, whipping dust into their wake. After two hours or so, the pick-ups turned off the road into the bush. Now there was just a rough track, no more road. As the pick-up bounced along the stoney surface, it listed severely side to side.

"If we don't have a flat tire we'll turn over for sure," laughed Dawit as he braced himself more firmly in the passenger seat.

"Guess it would be a good idea if I stop here for a few minutes and let's check the load," said JB. He climbed out first relighting his pipe and then inspected the lines. "It would be too much to ask you to pick-up the Hi-Lux I suppose if it turns over, huh . . . Dawit? So far it looks Ok! No flat yet!"

The pathway wove its way on to the crest of the mountain. From this point on it dropped steeply into a valley. Down below was the Burbur. JB changed the gears to four-wheel drive, checked the tires and the pick-up groaned its way down, stuttering on big rocks, skidding on the ever increasing damp soil. The air was now moist and humid. The soil turned to thick mud. JB shifted into first. The pick-up slithered its way down. Below was the gushing sound of the fierce Burbur, the greatly feared river which had not only taken many an Ethiopian life but those of some foreigners as well.

JB pulled the Hi-Lux over to level ground and stopped the engine. The soldiers riding in the accompanying Hilux had also arrived. As soon as they stopped, the soldiers dispersed around the pick-ups, their machine guns ready for action.

"What do you think Dawit," smiled JB, "no flats!"

"It is hard for me to believe," Dawit laughed.

"Now what?" JB mused.

"I think we just heave the rope to our party on the other side. Look, there they are," pointed Dawit.

The once Burbur Bridge was only rubble. But across the river were four Ethiopians and from what JB could see, four donkeys. Otherwise it was strangely quiet.

It took two and a half hours by the time they set up the pullies and had secured all the cartons of medicine hoisting them to the other side. At last there was just JB's old brown suitcase left. It was the same bag which he had used for all his world travels.

"Well, Dawit, thank you for all your help and your understanding. I could never have left Aguna without it."

"No problem. We understand the situation. There is little we can do about it, however. I think we are stuck with Vandenbos until he retires."

"But you could find a replacement, couldn't you?"

"There aren't too many foreign doctors who want to commit themselves to living in the bush of Ethiopia for many years. Most who would consider it have children and have to return home for their education or they are worried that after a few years that they will never get a job as a doctor when they return to the States or Europe. So, we are simply stuck with Vandenbos."

"A sad situation," commented JB. "I am really very, very sorry."

"Well, we are happy that you are going to Dabo Gatcho.

53

They have never had a doctor there and it is especially good at this critical time. We are grateful you will go there to help Sister Annemarie."

JB's suitcase was now on the other side. He tied the rope around his waist, shook hands with Dawit and pushed off from the river's edge. "Take care, Dr. Dawit, keep well and talk to us by radio. Don't forget us."

"OK, Dr. Bronson," Dawit said, waving as JB was pulled across.

All JB could hear was the enormous and powerful rush of the river as he slowly made his way to the other side. Who would believe that this is how I have to travel to another clinic here, he chuckled to himself.

"Welcome! Welcome! Dr. Bronson," said the Ethiopians as he touched down on the river's edge.

"Thank you for all your work," said JB untying himself. He turned and waved to Dawit on the distant shore.

"We have already sent two donkeys full of the packages up to the top. Our pick-up is at the top of the mountain. We cannot bring it down here you understand. It would never carry a load up this steep wet mountain side."

That night at about 9 PM, there was a standby between 36 and 95, Dabo Gatcho and Addis Ababa:

"95 do you read?" asked Sister Annemarie.

"Yes, 36. Catherine here."

"The white dove has arrived."

"This is good to know. I leave tomorrow for Germany," said Catherine.

"All the best 95."

"All the best to you all 36. Over and out!"

There were a few tears in Catherine's eyes. "I wonder when I will ever see him again . . . the white dove."

"Soon, I am sure," said Renate, Catherine's best friend. "We are trying not to give the military any unnecessary information about our activities as we can. If they all knew JB was going to Dabo Gatcho, for sure the medicine would have been intercepted. Of course, they would easily figure it out. We just try to camouflage it as best we can."

"Of course," Catherine said.

"But now you know he is there safe and you can enjoy your trip out of Ethiopia," Renate said. "It is so good to have you again in Addis. Tonight we have some delicacies to share with you, like cheddar cheese from Germany, a jar of pickles and a bottle of champagne."

"Paradise at last," chuckled Catherine taking her friend's arm and walking to the house. "I have so much to tell you."

"I thought you might," Renate smiled. "I know Aguna has not been an easy place."

"It is so nice for you to have me Renate. You cannot imagine what goes on there. It is really so wonderful to be here."

CHAPTER TWENTY-TWO

The Dabo Gatcho clinic had been built by Germans. It had a Bavarian style to it, varnished wood shutters, a second story with a balcony and wooden handrail. Sister Annemarie, a diaconic nun, was from Germany as well and could not help but decorate the second floor windows with numerous flower boxes. The Dabo Gatcho Clinic had a special reputation, not only for its pleasant architecture, but because of the 62 year old nun who was well-known for her compassion and sensitivity to the poor.

When JB arrived in the pick-up, Sister Annemarie, the clinic staff and many villagers were there to greet him. They had prepared a big village feast. As the pick-up slowed to a stop on the clinic compound, there was applause as JB opened the door.

"What's all this?" JB asked greeting Annemarie with a hug.

"It is the first time in all my 35 years out here that a doctor has come to work at this clinic. Welcome!"

"Well I am not sure it is worth all this celebration," JB smiled.

"How did you ever manage all these cartons of yours? The staff can bring them directly to your house," Annemarie explained as she surveyed the mountain of boxes on the back of the truck.

"Annemarie! This is all medicine! I arranged these supplies from Bodjii. My only belongings is that one little suitcase."

"Medicine! For us! Dr. Bronson, bless you, bless you," Annemarie said with excitement telling the staff in Oromo that the cartons were for the clinic.

As the weeks passed and the word got out there was plenty of medicine at the Dabo Gatcho clinic and there was now a doctor there as well, the number of daily patients increased from 200 to 350. The Sister and the Doctor became an ideal team. They were not the 9-5 missionary staff of the Aguna Hospital. The Dabo Gatcho clinic was open 24 hours a day. There was no discrimination, no one was denied admittance because of poverty or religion or tribe. All patients were welcome.

And on Sundays, they would take the pick-up and travel to neighboring villages to treat patients. And in the little spare time at Dabo Gatcho, JB was on the radio organizing convoys from

Addis to bring the shipments of medicine he arranged from the States.

One night as Annemarie and JB and one health assistant sat on the porch of her simple mud house, they discussed the fact that during the past week the number of patients treated each day had not been less 325.

"I'll write Helmut to send us two more health assistants. After all, we have more patients now per day than the entire Aguna Hospital."

Not surprisingly however, there was no answer to JB's request until one late afternoon when Ato Deresu appeared on the doorstep of Sister Annemarie's house.

"Annemarie! Look who is here! How are you Deresu?" inquired JB.

"So good to see you, Dr. Bronson!"

"Did Vandenbos send you to us?"

"No, I asked for a leave of absence from Aguna. Things there get worse. There is no medicine and Vandenbos gets angry at anyone who raises the idea of asking for your return. I heard a rumor that you needed help anyway," smiled Deresu.

"Well, Vandenbos should have no fear. I'd never return to Aguna. Dabo Gatcho with Annemarie is what I always dreamed of. And, Deresu, there are potatoes and mangos here," explained JB with a chuckle.

"So glad you are here, Deresu. You will love Dabo Gatcho. We have a perfect team here and you will make it more so," said Annemarie.

"But I left Aguna unofficially," explained Deresu.

"But you are officially welcomed at Dabo Gatcho," answered JB.

It was dinner time and as was the usual daily practice, the staff had congregated at Sister Annemarie's house to eat. There was no generator in Dabo Gatcho, no electricity and they sat by candlelight.

"We hear that you also take care of wounded soldiers," said Deresu.

"Of course, why not?" answered JB.

"At Aguna, Vandenbos refuses medical treatment for soldiers."

"We cannot refuse someone in need, Deresu. But treating the soldiers no matter what side they are on has its advantages. We are able to get medicine from Addis with little problem so far."

"Yea, so we hear. Aguna has no medicine left."

"I wonder if we will get a request from Aguna soon," laughed JB relighting his pipe.

"I don't think Vandenbos will ever dare to ask you to send him medicine," Ato Deresu laughed.

"What bothers me is that so many of these young soldiers are not in good health. I am very suspicious. I am afraid that many of them have HIV. Sister Annemarie and I have noticed all the symptoms."

"What are the symptoms?" Deresu asked.

"Well, so many are underweight, diarrhea is a common problem, they have swollen lymph nodes, constant fever. You will make rounds with me for the next few days, Deresu. I will point out all this to you then. You will become the expert."

CHAPTER TWENTY-THREE

Four months had passed and although Ethiopia was in critical turmoil, the remote village of Dabo Gatcho remained peaceful. The government soldiers and the OLF were not eager to disturb the clinic because they knew in time of need, they could depend on it for treatment.

Each evening JB and Annemarie would monitor the political situation on the BBC for a mere ten minutes to save their precious few batteries. Most of the missionaries had since left Aguna, packing their four-wheel drives and traveling south to Kenya. Ato Deresu had heard that most had flown home from Nairobi.

Though there had been great anticipation of the impending invasion of the opposition forces in Addis Ababa, it turned out not to be very violent. In fact, the EPRDF, the Eritreans, simply marched into town and as they did so, the dictator Mengistu Haile Mariam took off in a loaded aircraft for Zimbabwe where he was granted asylum.

During this time, however, the ever increasing evidence of HIV alarmed JB. He wrote a letter to the head office in Bodjii to let them know of his concern. He informed them that he and Annemarie were starting AIDS education and awareness at the Dabo Gatcho Clinic and encouraged them to do the same at Aguna and the other clinics as well. "Now that the civil war was over and thousands of soldiers were returning home to their families, it is a critical time for us to teach," JB advised the head office to see if they could get AIDS testing equipment for the clinics as well.

One afternoon, an unexpected truck drove into the compound of the Dabo Gatcho clinic. The driver unloaded a big carton.

"Mail! Can you imagine!" Sister Annemarie cried. "Finally, mail!"

JB and Annemarie spent most of that evening in silence, jut reading, the months of mail that had been finally delivered.

"Greetings from Catherine," JB told Annemarie smiling and tipping his chair back with a sigh of satisfaction.

"How is she?"

"Just fine and expecting to meet me in Addis soon since all is now peaceful.

"Uh, uh . . . here is a letter from Helmut."

"What does he write you for?" smiled Annemarie.

"To let me know that no AIDS testing equipment would be allowed out to any Church clinic or the Aguna hospital as long as he is the Chairman of the Medical Committee and that we are forbidden to teach about AIDS," JB continued to read, his voice tapering to a whisper.

"What is his reasoning. AIDS is simply a fact of life," Annemarie said, always baffled to hear what Vandenbos had to say.

"Look here . . . I have a letter from Dr. Dawit in Bodjii saying they will try to get some AIDS tests here and to go ahead and teach. Two different letters, one from the Chairman and one from the Vice Chairman of the same committee."

"And here, Annemarie. I have a letter from the President of the Church in Addis asking me to come to Addis soon. They would like me to take over a project there, an NGO to be exact, OSSA, the Organization for Social Services AIDS and develop a comprehensive AIDS program for all of Ethiopia."

"Wow! What shall I do?" JB asked, getting up from his chair to look up at the sky. "It has been so very wonderful here in Dabo Gatcho, a dream come true."

"For sure, that is no question. But you must go and start this program," said Annemarie. "This may be your ultimate task while in Ethiopia."

"But it has been so pleasant here in Dabo Gatcho."

"Yes, it was the nicest time for me as well. However, I agree with you that what we are seeing indicates a massive problem with AIDS for this country. You have a new call, Dr. Bronson.'

CHAPTER TWENTY-FOUR

It was 4:30 AM. JB secured the last ropes on the Hi-Lux. Ato Deresu would drive with him to Addis and then drive the pick-up back to Dabo Gatcho.

Sister Annemarie served coffee. "It hurts me to leave you," JB said, putting his hands around the warm cup.

"I've been out here alone most of my life. I'll manage though I'll miss your company and help for sure. It was so good to have you here during this civil war time. That is a direct blessing from God!"

"This Dabo Gatcho experience was the most wonderful of times in my entire career. It is what I have always dreamed of. Thanks Annemarie for having me here."

"Don't thank me. I believe truly God arranged it all. You have left me with many new and good ideas on how to improve this clinic."

"OK, then I will say . . . till later," and JB was off.

With his head full of sweet memories, JB and his companion Deresu pulled out of the Dabo Gatcho clinic compound under a star-studded sky. It was not far to the gravel road. In darkness, the pick-up slowly crawled through the crude path. By the time they reached the main road, there was the first glimpse of sunrise.

JB reflected on his experience as he followed the ever winding road to Addis, past the pastoral scenes unique to Ethiopia, the grass huts nestled into the landscape, the women in native dress, barefoot children walking to school, donkeys saddled with firewood and water.

He was about to trade his rural third-world experience for the city of Addis and yet he could not help but appreciate all he had learned from the simple countryside peasants of Ethiopia. Despite their poorness, they maintained a dignity, they were greatly thankful for any benefit that was offered to them. Theirs was a life infused with the spiritual, birth, life and death were all natural events. They had a connection with the earth as well as with the eternal. Then there were the foreigners, the missionaries, who instead of learning from these gentle people imposed "the short cut to heaven" in a most disenchanted form.

What had Lutheranism really brought them? Despite all, JB mused, despite Vandenbos and Aguna Hospital which in its crude way provided some good, there was room for so much improvement. It could do so much more and in a more sensitive way, with more civility.

As the hours passed, rural Ethiopia began to fade. Big trucks with long trailers fumed black smoke and clogged the highways. JB and Deresu closed the windows to avoid the foul air. On the outskirts of Addis, activity increased. In every direction there was movement. The pot-holed roads were alive with long files of donkeys heaped sky high with bundles of hay. Along the side of the road, young and old women were saddled with cumbersome loads of wood.

At one intersection, a man who supported two large mattresses on his head dodged across the street while a flock of goats followed in pursuit. Children were everywhere trying to play ball in any free part of the road they could find. Fruit stands lined the streets, vendors offered cheap watches, sunglasses, cigarettes and outmoded postcards. The taxis crowded the streets and did not follow any disciplined rules of the road. They seemed to assail the road in a precarious game of chance, darting out of line at any given time without signal.

Finally, after thirteen hours of driving. JB made a left turn into the mission guest house compound. He'd have a long hot shower, rest a little because tonight at 9 PM, Catherine would arrive at the airport. It had been seven long months since they had seen each other.

CHAPTER TWENTY-FIVE

The Lufthansa flight from Frankfurt made a dramatic swoop over Addis Ababa before landing. JB stood by the airport fence along with hundreds of others. No one was permitted inside the airport. Every movement was still restricted, the airport guards dressed in ragged army coats armed with sticks which they used without hesitation.

Having weathered the trying ordeal of customs, Catherine finally emerged pushing a wobbly cart piled high with luggage.

"Catherine!" JB shouted.

"JB!" Catherine cried trying to increase the speed of the disobedient old cart.

"Oh, Catherine," JB shoved through the crowd, his arms outstretched. "It has been so long."

"JB, it's so good to see you," as they stopped in the middle of the traffic to hug and kiss.

"Let's get out of here," JB said, taking over the navigation of the impossible cart, "before we too are beaten with those sticks." Crowds of young men grabbed at the luggage wanting to earn exorbitant tips for carrying the suitcases.

"This airport is a proper introduction to this country," Catherine said, glad to get inside the pick-up and to shut the door outside of which stood a cluster of beggars knocking on the window. "I don't think I can ever get used to it. There seems to be more beggars now than ever."

"They are ex-soldiers. They have no work, no livelihood. The worst thing for them is that the war is over," explained JB.

"But right now this is not my concern. Catherine, it is so good to see you," JB said as he leaned over to kiss her again. It's an hour since you landed. Don't things get any better inside with customs. After all, Ethiopia is now a democracy . . . supposedly."

"Well, I brought something decadent. They wanted to know why I brought this certain thing with me. I don't think we should bring it to the mission compound."

"For heaven's sake, what is it," JB asked smiling as he proceeded to drive out of the airport parking lot, the beggars still knocking on the windows.

"A bottle of champagne."

JB pulled the pick-up over to the side of the street. "Well, I do think we deserve a celebration. And I do agree with you, it would not be appropriate on the mission compound. Being the genius I am, I've booked ourselves a room at the most acceptable of hotels, well, as acceptable as can be found here. The Paradise Hotel to be exact! What do you think?"

"I think you did well," Catherine answered, stroking JB's arm. "But what's the surprise you said you had for me?"

"It is this," explained JB pulling back on the street, "we're not returning to the bush. I have a new assignment here in Addis."

"You're not serious!" Catherine screamed with excitement. "You mean we don't have to go back to Aguna?"

"I thought you might like that decision."

"Wow, I didn't guess that one at all!"

"Now you can be a lady of the city, you will have electricity, well most of the time, you can have a refrigerator, use a computer if you like, there will be a phone. Well, maybe most of the time!"

"And I could use the coffee machine!"

They pulled into the driveway of the Paradise Hotel.

"But what are you going to do in Addis, JB?"

"I'll be working for the NGO OSSA, the Organization for Social Services AIDS. It coordinates the AIDS activities and work in Ethiopia. The president of the Church has asked me to take this position and bring all the other Churches here together to make a unified program for Ethiopia. Later, I'm to try to get the Muslims involved as well."

"My goodness, what a job JB. Is this at all possible!"

"You know me, I will make it happen. Enough about work. Let's get to our room, and do more important things, like drink champagne."

CHAPTER TWENTY-SIX

The Paradise Hotel was the nickname for the Addis Ababa Hilton, now a thirty-year-old deteriorated building; but for those like JB who had come fresh out of the bush, it was a kind of paradise offering a hot shower, a TV and a room decor which was reminiscent of home.

"I suppose your first desire is the hot shower," giggled Catherine as they flopped on the beds of their fourth-floor room.

"I had one already on the compound in honor of your arrival," JB explained as he stretched out. "What's nice about the Paradise Hotel is that there should be less fleas here than elsewhere."

"Was your shower on the compound really hot?" Catherine continued giggling.

"No, nothing much has changed there since you left. The first thirty seconds were something like warm."

"Well, you now have three choices," Catherine laughed as she began to open the champagne. "You can have a hot shower, or a glass of this exquisite champagne or you could have . . . me."

"Uhm," laughed JB getting up off the bed. "I think it is not such a hard question," he explained as he took the bottle out of Catherine's hands. "After seven months, I know my priorities."

"I see."

"I think," and then JB scooped Catherine up and tossed her onto the bed kissing her deep and slowly. Their conversation stopped, there was an urgency as if they had just met again for the first time.

"Catherine, I missed you so."

"JB, it was far too long."

And they melted into each other as young lovers do.

They lay spent in each other's arms.

"There is something to be said for long separations," Catherine whispered.

"No, I don't think so," JB laughed, getting up to pour the champagne. "I don't like being alone so long. I really did miss you. Oh, this tastes good. One can forget," JB said as he downed a half a glass.

"How was Dabo Gatcho anyway?" Catherine asked as she sat up in the bed surrounded by pillows.

"It was what I had always dreamed of, the best time of my entire career. I was really free to help people and Annemarie and I worked together like a dream. But I do think that Ethiopia is in trouble."

"Why, now it has a new government?"

"Because I think that the returning soldiers are to a great percentage HIV positive. Now that they are home, they are infecting their wives and girl friends. It won't take long, Catherine, and how do you get the word out in a country where there is little communication system and where there is so much illiteracy. It will be a big challenge, this AIDS NGO. I'm not sure how successful we can be."

"Well, tonight you don't have to solve this problem. Now, let's take a hot shower together and then see if the Hilton has a good video on."

"Catherine, I first have to show you how much I missed you again," smiled JB.

66

CHAPTER TWENTY-SEVEN

"It is nice to sit by the pool. It is like the real or other world I used to live in," JB grinned. "This brunch looks good. What do you think?"

"I heard the Hilton has a new chef. Immodium is no longer needed," Catherine laughed.

"Well then, I will have scrambled eggs. So now tell me about the progress of your dissertation."

"It is done. My advisor, Dr. Beninger, from Princeton Theological suggested I write a psychological profile of Aguna and then design a program seminar or workshop I could theoretically offer to correct the situation," Catherine began to explain.

"Correct the situation? I thought you believed the only solution for Aguna was a gasoline bottle and a match," JB joked.

"Before that last resort," Catherine giggled, "I would first offer them a workshop. Of course, in reality, the mission would never ask me. You see their biggest problem is that they don't see that they have a problem. Because of this, the mission has developed into a kind of out of control evil machine. I think some missionaries are aware something is wrong with their work in Aguna, but it all starts at their headquarters in Mannesburg in Germany. To stop what is going on would mean closing down the mission headquarters in Mannesburg. It would mean loss of jobs. It is a cash factor that keeps it going. No one will speak up! They cover all their wrongness up with the theological excuse like saying 'we are just Christians and Christians are not perfect but God forgives us.' "

"And how did the mission get to be such an evil machine," JB inquired, relighting his pipe and sitting back into his chair.

"I found out that the Mannesburg Mission admits just about anyone into its seminary. You just have to say that you had 'a call from God' and you are in and what a deal! You get a nine-year free education as a missionary, free housing, free food, even a stipend to cover living expenses."

"And what happens after nine years?" JB asked.

"These students are then accustomed to a high standard of living. They have no worries. I learned that they are guaranteed a lifetime job forever. They have to complete the nine years in Mannesburg at the seminary, then they have to serve nine years abroad, somewhere in the third world. When they return to Germany they are then considered on an equal status as a theological graduate from the university; and what is interesting, they are always guaranteed a salary even if they can't be placed in a congregation somewhere. With that kind of career offer, many might think they heard a call from God. I think this is the crux of the problem. Applicants to this seminary are motivated by other reasons than compassion for those in need in the third world. A big part of the problem as I see it is that they do not get a university education. They never have exposure to a broad-minded study program. Instead they live in a small self-contained village and only among theologians of the missionary kind. It is a very narrow mind set.

I also learned that, compared to the theological department at a university, the Mannesburg Seminary is ill-staffed, dispenses an outdated system of education, the product of which comes to ordination half disciplined and with their vocation as missionary and theologian totally untested. The seminary routinely pumps the students up by giving them the illusion that a missionary is considered like some great white God in the third world. So their heads are fat but they are emotionally illiterate and these defective souls ultimately serve as role models for the Africans pointing out the short cut to heaven. Vandenbos first studied there then got his M.D. That explains a lot.

"We have certainly witnessed the result," JB added. "The true Biblical pharisees with not one clue as to what compassion is or how to help those in need."

"Exactly, but no one wants to stop this missionary machine because it means everyone could lose. These pastors in Mannesburg live very well, in nice big houses with a Mercedes in the driveway. The Mannesburg missionary gets more salary than you JB."

"I knew I had chosen the wrong profession."

"They don't like you because you don't comply with their rules and philosophy. You want to help the people and it makes them look bad so they hate us simple and clear."

CHAPTER TWENTY-EIGHT

"Are we really going to finish this brunch with champagne?"

"Why not! We can just go back upstairs and fall back into bed and go to sleep or," JB grinned as he stretched his arms in back of his head. "So tell me, what program did you design to help straighten the Mannesburg Mission out, this evil machine as you call it."

"Well, what you first need to know is that this mission has a very beautiful history," Catherine began as she sipped on her glass. "Its founder, a Ludwig Mann, was a pastor in a poor village later named Mannesburg after him. He wanted desperately to help his congregation because they were so poor and suffered so much. Mann had done a lot of study about Africa and then came up with the idea that he would start a missionary school and send his people out to Africa. In doing so, they would feel relief from their own suffering when they would encounter the African who was considerably worse off. His missionaries would then develop a sense of self worth as they started to help these less fortunate Africans. He taught his missionaries to go out to their assigned places in African and first build homes, schools and clinics for the Africans. His philosophy was that the African would be so overwhelmed with these wonderful missionaries that ultimately the African would be curious why he did all these good deeds. Only at that time would the missionary share the gospel with them.

"Unfortunately, the story with its unusual philosophy seems to have gotten lost after 250 years. Mannesburg first needs to revive it. You can say that the Mannesburg Mission has made a success of Christian Mission, but not of Christianity. It started with very little money but now is the recipient of large donations which as you know does not always reach its ultimate destination. Look at your AIDS work!

"Yes, even though I do the fundraising the money all goes directly to the mission. Even if I have collected it!" JB added, "But when I need it I sometimes have to fight to get at it. You remember when they did not release the money I collected for my seminar in Nekemte. Remember we had to take our own savings to get the money in time!"

"How could I ever forget!" said Catherine, her eyes narrowing with a surge of emotion. "But it isn't only the money, it is the prestige. When I was in Mannesburg on my way back here I was at lunch at the seminary. Some teacher, a theologian, got up after the meal and told the students just what a great status they would have when they go to Africa as a missionary, that everyone will look up to them. On top of that they publish a Mannesburg Magazine which further puffs up all their missionaries, the theologians of course.

"Like I said before Mannesburg is certainly successful in the business of Christianity, but not successful in promoting the message I think Christ intended, that being just simple kindness to one and all," Catherine added.

"And your explanation?" JB smiled as he relit his pipe and turned his face towards the warm sun.

"Simply this, that the Mannesburg Theological Doctrine is that you love the Divine Father and therefore are the recipient of salvation and God's forgiveness. They don't feel accountable for their personal actions towards others. Their behavior is left up to God to judge. They are assured forgiveness in any event. No matter what sorrow or hurt they produce, their actions are of no consequence. There is no motivation to make every word you speak one of peace, every action one of compassion, every gesture one of harmony. Do you understand what I mean?

"So my program, the Aguna Program," Catherine paused looking at JB and laughing, "introduces a Christian approach to karma, emphasizing that Christianity is not just Bible study but is expressed in one's very actions, minute to minute. It explores new iconic metaphors for the mission, focusing on the idea to minister and not be ministered to. It would teach the missionaries to use every conflict as a source of personal or organizational growth rather than reason for attack. It focuses on the nature of relationships and team work. I use the Bronsons as an example throughout the program," Catherine concluded. "What do you think of that?

"Well," JB grinned, then chuckled, "it has been interesting to do. I have learned a lot and it has been a good therapy for me. Your advice to turn the 'scars of the Aguna experience into a star' was the best advice ever. What is still hard to accept is that Mannesburg continues to disillusion so many of its co-workers, but more importantly its continued behavior poisons the Ethiopians and they have enough problems with daily life without anyone adding more.

"The very scary thing is that you and I are a part of the small handful of people who actually see what is going on and JB, there is something else which concerns me. A secretary at Mannesburg pulled me aside, JB. She told me she heard that we knew what was going on and that we might be prone to talk about it to outsiders. She cautioned me to be very careful that Mannesburg has its way to silence people. Do you believe that?"

"Well, yes, now I do," JB added with reflection. "Come to think about it, there is a clause in my contract which forbids me to make public any details of what goes on inside this mission. I never gave it too much thought at the time. Now I can fully understand their anxiety."

"But I have never signed a contract with them JB!" Catherine said aggressively. "I could be threatening to them, couldn't I?"

"Yes, I suppose so. Let me give this some thought Catherine. What you have heard from this secretary is certainly an eye-opener," JB suggested with a certain look of concern.

"Enough of this subject, JB. Let us go and take a nap," Catherine said as she took JB's hand. "It is a sad subject. If I were to talk about it to the outside world, people wouldn't like to hear it. The mission would be angry and take some sort of revenge, probably painting me as a true un-Christian. But on the other hand there is a responsibility for someone to speak up and say that this is not what is needed in the way of international help for Africa. They have enough problems."

CHAPTER TWENTY-NINE

JB pulled his new OSSA Landcruiser into the parking lot of the downtown Ras Hotel. He was to meet his Ethiopian OSSA counterpart, Ato Girma. The Landcruiser purred to a stop. It was such a change from the old beaten pick-ups used in the mission. The seats were well upholstered, it had an extra big fuel tank for long distance driving and even a working radio. One can get spoiled for sure, JB mused with a smile as he locked the trunk.

"Hello, Doctor," said Ato Girma, a short plump Ethiopian with a friendly sincere smile.

"Ah, Ato Girma," JB answered as he walked over to shake his hand.

"You had no trouble finding this place?"

"No, Ato Girma, your instructions were so good. I'm getting to know my way around in Addis in just a few days. It's not easy. There are no street signs anywhere and no good map of this city."

The two men walked down the steps into the lounge of the Ras chatting about the onset of the rainy season.

"Do you like our native dish, Doctor?"

"Very much. But I've been eating it every day for the last few months. We had no foreign food out in Dabo Gatcho. So I think I'm going for a pasta dish for a change."

The two men exchanged polite conversation about their families, but slowly their focus was directed to the business of AIDS.

"This new transitional government is very quiet about the AIDS problem. It is not a priority at all with them. Their first agenda is to establish themselves as a long-term government. You know Doctor, there are many of us who don't think the Americans did us any favor at London. Your Mr. Cohen put them in power. We can only hope for the best," Ato Girma explained. "I'm not sure of what we can count on as far as support for our AIDS work."

"I realize the situation. I was at the American Embassy just yesterday. They still think this government is the best chance for Ethiopia. Of course, the bottom line is to keep Ethiopia peaceful, not letting it slip into another Somalia. So far, so good, the

72

Embassy people think, but I realize we must wait and see. Time will tell. But what does the AIDS situation look like to you now?"

"I think at least 35-40% of the sexually active population could be infected with HIV. I cannot publicly say that. We can get away by saying 15%, but we could get into serious trouble from the Ministry of Health. If you ask the doctors here what they are seeing, they will tell you 80% of the patients admitted are HIV infected. In Bahir Dar I heard a report that 17% of a group of pregnant women tested were HIV positive. They apparently did the test a second time with another group of women and 19% tested positive."

"What about the prostitutes in the city here? I have heard there are as many as 280,000 in Addis alone."

"We did some testing secretly and found 90% positive," said Ato Girma pausing from his lunch with a look of grave concern.

"I am worried that a great percentage of the returning soldiers who came to the clinic for treatment in Dabo Gatcho were HIV positive. It was a real shock. I then started to write as many letters as possible to supposed authorities to let them know this." JB explained with solemn tone.

"Of course, we also have a big refugee problem on the Sudan as well as Somalia borders, Doctor. We will also be responsible for the AIDS situation in these camps. That in itself is enough to cope with," Girma added.

"We will have to build OSSA up as fast as we can. Time is essential when it comes to the AIDS problem. We have to train counselors and establish branch offices throughout Ethiopia as fast as we possibly can."

CHAPTER THIRTY

It was a yellow building with dark red shutters. Banana trees surrounded the house on its balcony; it had a swinging chair. "This is where I hope to spend my time," JB laughed to his staff. Everyone chuckled for they knew already that if their project advisor could find a house and compound for OSSA in three days time, he was not the kind to rest on the swing of the front porch.

"I think the photocopier had better go over here, Ato Girma," suggested JB, eyeing the partial hole in the ceiling.

"Ah, I see what you mean Doctor. It does not look so good up there." Parts of the roof leaked but still it was the best house they could find in such a short period of time. "We will have to take our chances with this ceiling," Ato Grima chuckled.

"This room should be your office, Girma," directed JB as they slowly walked their way in and out of the house before they moved in their meager collection of furniture.

"Oh, Doctor, no. Where are you going to sit? No, no, this room is for you."

"Absolutely not. This is the office of the General Manager of OSSA. I am just your Advisor. I will sit out here with the pretty secretaries."

"Oh, Doctor. I'm not sure. You're the foreigner. The foreigner always gets the best office."

"Not this time, Ato Girma. It's settled.

"Enough work! Let's go and get a coffee," JB said, pausing to relight his pipe.

The two men walked across the street to a small "bunabet," a coffee shop. They sat outside underneath an umbrella. Addis Ababa had boomed with small outdoor coffee shops since the change in government.

"I have a promise of three containers of medicine from the States," began JB. "We can keep the containers as well and I was thinking we could use them on our compound for storage. I am working on getting seven more that we could use for starting our branch offices. We would have to decide which places have priority."

"Doctor, you are quite amazing. You have only been with us

for two weeks."

"Oh, that's not all, Girma. I have a promise of two computers, one more photocopier, a fax machine, and seven desks, chairs, cabinets as well."

"Who would give us all that?" asked Ato Girma, his head tilted with curiosity.

"My old medical practice is moving. They are buying all new equipment for their new office, so I just told them they must send all their old equipment to Ethiopia. It only took them five minutes for them to answer with an OK. They will pay the shipment costs as well."

* * *

"Doctor JB, there you are! Some young people have come to the office. They said they would like to talk to you if you have the time," explained Alemnesh, the secretary.

Outside the office stood twelve or so young men. As JB approached, one of the young men extended his hand and introduced himself as Ato Solomon. "Are you Dr. Jack?"

"Well, yes and who are all of you? We don't have more than five chairs here. We didn't expect a visit yet of more than twelve people."

"We couldn't wait to come and see this OSSA and we heard that a Dr. Jack might be of help to us. We represent a group of young people here in Addis. We meet every week and discuss this disease called AIDS. We have already seen many of our friends die of this strange thing. We tried to get help for our club, some training. We went to the Ministry of Health, but they said they could not help us. Then last week someone told us of OSSA and a Dr. Jack."

"Let us go inside. How nice for you to come. Of course, we will help you, that is why we are here."

As the twelve young men sat on the floor, JB listened to them intently. He had never seen such enthusiasm before. The young people wanted to take action, they wanted to go out and teach other young people about the hazards of this disease.

"Do you have an office?" asked JB.

"An office, oh no," laughed Ato Abebe, the group's vice-president. Doctor, we have no resources for such an expense. We just meet at different homes."

"Well, now you have an office. It is here, you start in that corner."

The eyes of the young men got big and round as they stared at each other with disbelief.

"What do you call your group?"

"We were thinking of calling it SAVE YOUR GENERATION."

CHAPTER THIRTY-ONE

JB pulled his Landcruiser into a parking space designated "visitor." He had a nine o'clock appointment with His Holiness, the Abune Paulos, the Patriarch of the Ethiopian Orthodox at the Tewahedo Church. It seemed like another world, the priests and their long and sometimes very colorful robes, their gilded Ethiopian crosses. JB felt a tinge of anticipation.

"Dr. Bronson," greeted a handsome priest. "I am Father Daniel. I am to take you to His Holiness."

"Thank you, that would be most helpful," JB replied, studying the flowing black garment, the black cap and brilliant cross which hung around the priest's neck.

"We think your work with OSSA will help us all in Ethiopia with this AIDS disease. At least we sincerely pray for this, Doctor," explained the priest as they both walked across the parking lot to another building. "We can only help as much as the Churches are willing to be open to this entire question of AIDS. How open is the Patriarch?" JB dared to ask.

"I think you will like His Holiness. He is quite open to all subjects."

They had climbed five flights of stairs. "Let me go in now and announce your presence," said the priest.

JB sat in a simple room, the walls a faded green with two old plastic red chairs, a table with old church newsletters in Amharic and a copy of the latest *ADDIS ABABA TRIBUNE* featuring JB's picture with title: "Project Advisor for OSSA says 'we must all fight AIDS together'." *The Addis Tribune* was edited by a well-traveled Ethiopian, a man who had been educated in the US. JB hoped the editor would not be the brunt of unnecessary trouble having featured the article on the first page.

"Dr. Bronson," a pretty young woman said, "you may come in now."

JB entered a large room at the end of which sat the black-robed Abune Paulos sitting on a red velvet, gold-leafed chair. He immediately got up saving JB the necessity to go through any uncomfortable formality. "How nice you make this visit to us Doctor. Let us sit over here." The Patriarch pointed to a cluster of worn sofas and chairs in the corner of an adjacent room.

"How have you found our country?" began the Abune Paulos with a friendly and relaxed tone. "I hear you have worked extensively in the west with the Evangelical Church and their mission hospital. I sometimes have found that foreigners who come to work for the Evangelical Church have no idea about the Ethiopian Orthodox Church and our history. Have you ever visited any of our Orthodox Churches in Addis or have you been to Axum or Lalibella?" the Patriarch questioned.

"I'm a simple doctor, Your Holiness. I want to help save as many here in Ethiopia from AIDS as possible. Yes, I have worked in the west with the missionaries but I am not hesitant to say, that after this experience, that I could never consider myself a missionary. It was in someways a very disappointing experience for me with the exception of my time in Dabo Gatcho where I worked with a saintly diaconic nun," JB explained, aware of the Patriarch's uncomfortableness.

The Abune Paulos smiled. It was a look of relief that the new project advisor for OSSA was not a religions fanatic of the missionary variety he had encountered, those who were so sure that they and they only were recipients of the true gospel.

The hard and relatively unknown fact was that the Lutherans had chosen to ignore the Orthodox Church in Ethiopia concentrating rather on the building of their own religious kingdom within the country. Billions of dollars came into the country in support of their activities leaving the Orthodox Church on its own. It was the cause of hard feelings and Dr. Bronson was now well aware of it having realized that in the so-called preparation course in Mannesburg, Germany, which he and Catherine were required to attend before leaving for Aguna, there had been no discussion nor mention of the Orthodox Church and its rather spectacular history.

"I may have received the offer from the Evangelical Church to take this position with OSSA," explained JB, "but my task is to work with all the Churches within Ethiopia on the topic of AIDS. Not any one Church will have preference, Your Holiness."

They continued to talk, each growing in respect for the other.

"If you would supply me with a helicopter," said the Abune with a chuckle, "I would fly all over Ethiopia and teach about AIDS," he laughed. "The question is always transportation and costs for training priests who are knowledgeable about AIDS. We don't have the support the Lutherans have."

"I have an idea, Your Holiness," JB began. "What if we bring the heads of all Churches in Ethiopia together to talk about AIDS. What if we have a big conference in Sodere, south of here and we invited the leaders of the Churches and upper staff to begin a discussion about how we are going to approach the AIDS pandemic. I am thinking of arriving at a common statement at the end of the conference for all the Churches together."

His Holiness leaned over. His eyes sparkled. "Dr. Bronson, that is a most convincing plan. You have my complete support. I will even come for the conference myself and I will send my top priests to attend the full length of this conference."

JB left the Orthodox Church headquarters encouraged by the open attitude of its Patriarch and went straight to OSSA. His mind buzzed with ideas, plans and the amount of work which would have to be done. He needed to talk immediately with Ato Girma.

* * *

"We . . . I mean, you, are already famous, Dr. Jack," Ato Grima said.

"We," answered JB. "And famous for what?"

"The Ministry of Health has requested an invitation for this Sodere Conference."

"An invitation! Is this a good sign. They should come, but I am surprised since it is a conference for the Church staff only."

"They might be afraid," suggested Ato Girma, afraid of not having complete control over the AIDS work, afraid that another organization like the Churches would set policy."

"The government is not the only one who seems to be afraid. My organization, this mission, I came out to Ethiopia with . . . they will not send any of their pastors to participate in this conference. I think they are also afraid, afraid that the Catholics, the Orthodox and the Evangelicals will fight against each other and the conference will be a total failure and they don't want to be associated with any failures."

"Oh, Doctor, I forgot to give you this message. A friend of yours called to let you know that a Dr. Helmut Vandenbos wants to come. He wants to introduce his book on AIDS."

"His book on AIDS!" JB gasped, leaning way back in his chair. What could Helmut write about AIDS? He had denied its existence before. He had forbidden me even to talk or teach about it.

"Well, on second thought, let him have a part of the agenda, I guess. Perhaps he has come to his senses regarding the AIDS issue," explained JB.

CHAPTER THIRTY-TWO

A four-car convoy slowly entered the gate of Sodere which in years past had been an Orthodox Retreat, a site of holy waters and healing. The communist dictator, Menguistu, had taken control of it, opening it to the general public.

The entourage of black-gowned priests assembled around the Patriarch carrying their golden crosses, bronze-tipped prayer sticks and briefcases. His Holiness made a slow and gracious exit from the back seat of his limo. He greeted JB without hesitation. "You know, Doctor," he whispered, "we must fast till 1 PM. I hope this does not interfere with your lunch schedule today."

"We are aware of this Your Holiness. Please come inside. We have a table waiting for you where you can wait till your lunch hour."

As they walked to the reception area, cameras flashed; a crowd of videos documented the event.

"Perhaps, I will first talk to the press for you, Doctor," said His Holiness.

"This would be very helpful for us," answered JB, pleased at the openness and obvious political acumen of the Patriarch.

His Holiness sat in a corner chair surrounded by his colorful bishops. The journalists scurried setting up their equipment and an interview began with a flood of pointed questions.

"Your Holiness, what do you think the role of the Church is in teaching about AIDS?"

"Your Holiness, what do you think about the use of condoms?"

"Your Holiness, what about sex outside of marriage?"

The Catholic Cardinal had now arrived as well. Father Yohannes walked briskly up to JB. How are things so far, Doctor?" he asked.

The President of the Evangelical Church pulled up in his four-wheel Mercedes Benz. He modestly stepped out of his car, walked in and greeted the Patriarch who caught his arm saying, "Brother Tesfi, sit with me. Let us talk to the press together."

That evening the Patriarch had invited the two hundred participants to walk with him to the small Orthodox Church on the hill outside of Sodere. The sun was about to set, the sky was aflame with color, bright stars began to glitter like angels. The priests started to chant, incense was heavy in the air and His Holiness welcomed all, setting a harmonious tone for the conference.

The next morning JB welcomed the guests on behalf of OSSA. "Fifteen years ago the word 'AIDS' was not really known. Today, millions of people are sick with AIDS, millions have already died and an estimated 20 million people in the world are infected with the virus. Because there is no cure as of yet, the infected people will also die of AIDS. It is predicted that by the year 2,000, a mere five years from now, an estimated 120 million people will be infected. We are here this week to unite the Churches of Ethiopia in the fight against AIDS. Without the help of the Churches we cannot predict much success. Ethiopia is one of the most spiritual countries in the world. The Churches can reach the people," JB continued, dressed in a white shirt and tie.

During the short coffee break that followed, the young men from SAVE YOUR GENERATION huddled around JB.

"You're next, Solomon!" JB grinned.

"OK, Doctor, I will do my best."

* * *

"Good morning! My name is Solomon. I am the president of SYGA, SAVE YOUR GENERATION. It is an anti-AIDS club. Our sole purpose is to teach the youth of this country about AIDS, to help them save their generation. Dr. Jack has asked me to introduce SYGA to you so that you know of our existence, so that you can refer young people from your Churches to join us and be a part of our organization. We do dramas and street plays and songs about AIDS. Today, we brought three young people from your organization with AIDS experiences to talk to you," Solomon concluded, looking to JB for approval.

First, a young woman named Tigist spoke. She was a poor orphaned girl who had turned to prostitution to make a living. "I now have AIDS. I work now with OSSA. I go everywhere with Dr. Jack and his team to talk about this disease. I am so thankful to find OSSA. They gave me counseling about AIDS and I also found a new life. I have also found Jesus after I got AIDS. I now tell everyone to find help and learn about AIDS before it is too late."

Secondly, a young man, a former soldier, told his story. It was brief. "I was a soldier. I got AIDS. My family does not want me anymore. No one wants me anymore. Most of the time I am quite sick. I tried to go to the Church to find help. No one wanted to talk to me. You pastors must help people like us. We did not know about this disease before. I had been sleeping on the street until I met OSSA and Dr. Jack. Now I am a teacher about AIDS. I want to say we need to have the help of the Church and you pastors. Don't turn your back on us."

The conference hall became quiet as a third, a young boy, began to speak. "I do not have AIDS, but my mother and father died of it. I have six brothers and sisters I must now take care of. I am fourteen years old. The entire day, I am taking care of my sisters and brothers. I am washing the clothes, cooking and shopping. I am doing what a mother and father do. I don't have time to go to school. I now have help from OSSA. But I want to tell you . . ." the boy's voice faded. Tears flowed from his eyes. The conference room was stone silent. Then JB noticed that many of the pastors in the audience themselves were crying.

"Please, help us, the small ones who have no father, no mother anymore. I cannot go to school and it was my dream. We need your help. OSSA says there will be many, many children like me."

The next morning in Addis Ababa the first edition of the *MONITOR* read:

"Physician Urges Clerics To Give Sex Education."

ETV, the Ethiopian Television, presented portions of the conference on the nightly news.

Overnight Dr. Jack Bronson had become known as the "Crusader" against AIDS. He had become a household name.

CHAPTER THIRTY-THREE

The guest speakers invited to speak at Sodere had included such names as Dr. Robert Schuller of the Crystal Cathedral, sports hero and now AIDS infected Magic Johnson. It was understandable that their busy schedules prohibited their attendance but they both were kind enough to offer letters of encouragement for the mission of Sodere.

In contrast, however, were the Mannesburg missionary pastors who professed to be so interested and involved in Ethiopia but were too busy to attend. They did not offer any support for Sodere which made JB suspicious. They were simply afraid, he concluded, afraid that the conference would fail, afraid the various denominations would end up fighting amongst each other and that no common statement would be reached. These pious pastors did not want to take the risk of being associated with possible failure though this was clearly a job for them, to bring together the Christian community in Ethiopia; this was a project that could really help Ethiopia. But they were afraid, afraid of making statements about use of condoms, to explain the Biblical implications and JB knew that many of them believed that AIDS was a disease, a punishment by God for the unrighteous. In a way, thought JB, they probably silently hoped Sodere would not turn out to be a success either. If it did . . . then they would not be a part of it, they could not claim the success.

As the days passed, JB observed that at meal times the pastors were talking with each other, the different denominations were sitting with each other, real dialogue was taking place.

Dr. Jim from England was one of the brave foreigners who did not hesitate to accept an invitation to speak at the Sodere Conference. His specialty was psychotherapy, his specialty sexuality. The clergy hung on his every word. For sure, the pastors of Ethiopia had rarely if ever heard such openness on the subject. Dr. Jim, a quite handsome tall man, spoke from the podium:

"If we only see sexuality in terms of biology, then we will see it as the act of sexual intercourse between two people. If we only see it in terms of pleasure, then often in our male dominated society it will be seen in terms of the pleasure given to men. What we need is to endeavor to see it as a relationship between two equal people. This is enormously important for us as Christians and needs to be a core part of our message. As St. Paul says, there is no distinction between freeman and slaves, between Jew and Greek, between man and woman. Man and woman have been made in the image and likeness of God and we know that our God is a God who relates, the Father, the Son and the Holy Spirit. This is what Jesus came to teach us, the way that the Father relates with each of us and how we can respond. Jesus promises that the Father and Himself will come to make their home in us. Jesus is inviting us to experience the kind of relationship that He is having with the Father and the Spirit. I believe that this is very important for us to hold on to. And it challenges us as men to change our attitudes to our beliefs about women.

"If women are not equal in our relationships then our relationships are not God-like and we need the courage and the faith to question ourselves about that and to change.

"Sexuality is about relationships, relationships between two people who love one another. Let me just say this in passing: I have listened to you this week talking about prostitution in Ethiopia and how a stop could be put to the spread of HIV/AIDS if all the prostitutes were rounded up and locked away. But may I ask you a question? Why do men need prostitutes? Why is that question never put to men? Why does that question not surface in this meeting? It is like anything else on the market; if there is no demand there will be no produce. If men did not need the services of these women then the women would lose their trade. But we never hear about men being challenged by such a question, do we? It is so much easier to blame the women, to put the cause of it all on them. Just like Adam did, I suppose, and just like the Scribes (all men) did when they brought the woman caught in adultery to Jesus. Why was the man not also brought to Jesus? Was he not committing sin too? Our sexual relationships, our sexuality, therefore is a gift of God and it is one of the most intimate acts of ourselves as human beings. It is about intimacy.

"That word Intimacy . . . when we hear it, we quite often think that it is about genital intimacy. We frequently begin to think of intimacy in terms of our genitalia. But intimacy is much more than that. Intimacy is about the way we relate, it is about our feelings and our emotions, it is about the way we touch and are touched by others. And it is also about our genitals, about those parts of our bodies also given by God that allow us to rejoice in the gift of our sexuality.

"Very often in our male dominated world, we miss out on the emotional side. How difficult it is for us men to be

83

emotional, to let the soft side of ourselves be seen. I can remember as a little boy being told to 'grow up' or 'be a man' whenever I shed a tear. We miss out on the expressions of these most important parts of our psyche as men, our emotions, our feelings of sadness, of joy, of anger.

"Somehow, these emotions are not allowed to be shown. And I see quite a lot of that in my work as a counselor among priests especially among celibate priests. Often they find it particularly hard to let their emotions be seen by others, they are fearful that by showing their emotions, they might get out of control and something might happen, something that may threaten their way of life. And this can be sad.

"If we avoid intimacy because we are afraid of it . . . we avoid it in certain ways like isolation and promiscuity. If I have relationships that are sexual then I can avoid being intimate with any one of them. I can avoid the 'one to one' relationship. The more we study men and women who act like this, the more we see that what these people are vainly searching for is intimacy with another person and yet are so terrified of such intimacy that they never remain long enough with one person for it to happen.

"And this is important in our effort to change our behavior in relationship with the spread of HIV/AIDS. Promiscuity is one of the sure ways of spreading HIV. What are we looking for in our promiscuous behaviors? We will avoid promiscuity not only by proclaiming the law and the teaching of God, but we also must understand our natures and the way we are made up psychologically. That will also help us to understand why it is that we seek promiscuity rather than the one to one relationship that God intends for all of us."

Dr. Jim bowed his head slightly and the audience of pastors broke into a loud and standing applause. JB's eyes began to tear as he joined in the applause. He could not have had a better speaker. It was the best of presentations. The conference thus far was a success.

CHAPTER THIRTY-FOUR

On the last day of the conference, the press jammed the center front of the conference hall. They were anxious to cover the "Final Common Statements By All Churches In Ethiopia" for the AIDS Challenge.

"The Preface," began one of the Orthodox Bishops, "God has created us in His image and likeness. This means that we were created and sanctified with God's holiness, not of sickness, but health, not to be sad, but to be happy, not to die, but to live. However, though our forefathers could not keep the blessings and dignity they received from God. They became slaves for sin. But God so loves us, he sent his only son to save us. He freed us from the bondage of sin.

"However, our history shows us that the various problems have challenged humanity. The disease of our time, AIDS, is no different from the severe problems that presented a challenge to mankind in the past. Though the cause of AIDS is not yet clear, the problem gives pastors and priests the challenge to be involved in the fight against the disease and give the necessary care to patients. The disease also gives a chance for people to confess their sins, come closer to God and receive His glory by obeying His law of love.

"We, the participants of this workshop," the Bishop concluded, "organized by OSSA, an organization which understands the extent of this pandemic, are and will continue to discuss the issues raised in the workshop."

This common statement is what Dr. Jack Bronson had hoped for. It provided a commitment from all the Churches to educate pastors about AIDS, to design common teaching programs to teach about AIDS. It provided a common policy for the care of people infected with AIDS, it provided a commitment to support OSSA in its evolving work with AIDS within the country.

As the Bishop finished reading the statement, there was applause and a true feeling of euphoria in the room. Pastors hugged each other.

"Dr. Bronson, this could not have happened without you," said the Patriarch. "You have done a great thing not only for AIDS but for the Churches of Ethiopia. It is the first time we have come together to talk to each other. Few people were willing to think that this conference could be a success."

Unfortunately, however, the conference was not over. There was still the rest of the day, its closing and Dr. Helmut Vandenbos who had insisted for time to address the audience. He arrived in a four-wheel drive just after lunch. The pastors were just getting seated.

"I have brought the Minister of Health with me," Helmut snapped as he walked passed JB and without hesitation taking his place at the podium. "Good afternoon my fellow believers. I am Dr. Helmut Vandenbos from the Aguna Hospital in Wollega. I want to tell you the truth about AIDS. I have news for you all," Helmut began with abruptness. "Dr. Bronson is not telling you the truth about AIDS. He is trying like so many in this world to undermine the Churches, to get us to talk about those issues which should not be talked about. You know what I mean, I refer to sex, premarital sex and the sin of condoms. The truth is that 97% of the persons who have HIV in their bodies, were purposely infected with this virus which can lead to AIDS."

Catherine, who had been standing in the far corner of the conference hall, felt a sudden weakness in her knees as she listened. She quickly glanced at JB to see that same ashen gray color in his face which she had first seen in Aguna, the day Helmut refused to operate on the wounded young man. She felt almost faint.

"HIV is supplied to them through vaccines, drugs, blood transfusions, and food, by HIV containing microbes in drinking water and by insects. It is all here in my book. You can buy it if you want. I brought 500 editions here. If you cannot afford the 150 Birr cost, I will donate it to you so you can learn the truth. Now that the Ministry of Health has read this book and believes it, they have decided that there will be no more need for teaching about AIDS, no more reason for OSSA, no more reason for Dr. Bronson or this kind of conference."

JB gasped, grabbing the side of his chair as he tried to stand. His face suddenly turned deep grey. He clutched his chest. His face grimmaced in severe agony and pain. And then as he struggled to his feet, he staggered, then winced and fell over. Catherine screamed. The audience stood up in horror. Someone cried for a doctor.

Dr. Vandenbos did not move. He just watched the crowd encircle JB who now lay on the floor. Helmut's mission was successful and complete.

CHAPTER THIRTY-FIVE

"He has had a heart attack," explained Dr. Tekeste, an Ethiopian doctor, friend and support of OSSA. "We have to get him to Addis as soon as possible. There is nothing here we can do for him. There is no hospital here, no medicine. Let's get a car ready for him, the most comfortable one for transportation."

"He rides in our limousine," said the Patriarch. "Let us put him inside now and begin as fast as we can to Addis."

Catherine hovered over JB. He opened his eyes. His face was still gray. He tried to smile. "It was almost a success," he said. "At least, I tried to do something for AIDS here." Then he closed his eyes. Catherine wept softly.

In minutes, JB was carefully carried into the back seat of the limousine. The crowd of shocked pastors hovered around him. "He is our dear father," said one young priest; "he is what we need here in Ethiopia. I don't understand why this has to happen to someone so fine. We will pray for him."

"He needs rest, Catherine," said the doctor. "It is best you ride in one of the four-wheel drives. I will ride with him in the limo."

The three-car convoy sped towards Addis, the pot-holed roads causing discomfort and pain as JB lay in the back seat of the limousine. The two-lane road was full of trucks and the driving was erratic, the ride seemed endless for Catherine.

As the Patriarch's limousine drove up to the entrance of the Black Lion, the biggest and reportedly best hospital in Ethiopia, a crowd instantaneously gathered around. Why, was the Patriarch's limousine at the hospital? Was something wrong with the Abune Paulos?

At first the hospital could not find a stretcher on which to transport JB. Secondly, there was no available room for him in the intensive care ward! For an hour, nothing seemed to happen. Finally, the Patriarch was able to negotiate a temporary make-shift bed for Dr. Bronson in the corner of the over-crowded intensive care ward. But this was only the beginning of the nightmare for Catherine.

There were no bed sheets, no cover, and to Catherine's horror, no medicine. No pain relievers! Catherine began to run after staff and ask what next, doesn't a doctor come? What about medicine? Are there no nurses to help here?"

"Here," one doctor abruptly said, "this is a list of the medicine your husband needs."

"What do you mean?" Catherine asked shaking.

"This is the medicine he needs now as soon as possible," the abrupt doctor shouted to Catherine.

"Where do I get it, where is your pharmacy?" she asked.

"We have none. We have no medicine here, Miss. You have to get it wherever you can find it here in Ethiopia," the doctor replied, looking at Catherine with indifference, as an example of a typical foreigner expecting too much. The doctor then turned away without any emotion and went to the next bed.

Catherine began to cry just as she surveyed the ward, its chipped painted walls, foul smell, lack of decor, lack of organization.

Then Ato Solomon, the young president of the SYGA appeared. "Don't cry Catherine! Us boys will go around to every pharmacy and see what we can get for our dear Dr. Jack."

"You will need money. Let me see if JB has any in his brief case."

She looked at JB who now lay on an uncomfortable bed. His chest heaved up and down. She stumbled across his briefcase, her hands shaking as never before in her life, in disbelief over the conditions of the medical care. "Here Solomon, here is 1000 Birr."

"We will also get bed sheets, a pillow and a cover from our houses; we will also try to find a nurse for him. We will get someone from OSSA to come and take care of him."

"Aren't there any nurses in the hospital, Solomon?"

"No, Catherine, one has to get all these things oneself here."

"And this is the best hospital in Ethiopia?" Catherine winced. "I suppose I thought it would be at least as good as a mission hospital."

The boys raced off. Meanwhile, no one came to JB's bedside. The doctors were all too busy to come. "It is worse than any nightmare I could dream of," Catherine sobbed to herself. "If only he could get pain killer."

Just then, to the horror of Catherine, the young man in the next bed screamed. Two doctors stood around him not doing much. Then she heard one say, "He is dead."

As Catherine looked around the intensive care ward, she gasped at the horror that several patients lay dead in the beds, completely covered.

"Why was such a horror happening to JB after all the good he tried to do. The hours seemed to drag on while Catherine tried to make JB feel as comfortable as she could.

Finally, Ato Solomon and his friends returned. They had

found four of the seven needed medications.

"You go home now, our car waits for you outside. We will call you if we need you. We will stay with him all night. At least we got the pain killer. We brought with us everything we need. Here, we even have water for him."

"You have to also provide your own food and water?" Catherine asked, now totally numb and not interested in the answer.

"I tried my best to get medicine for Dr. Jack," Dr. Tekeste whispered in Catherine's ear. "I went to your Mannesburg Mission to ask. They should have some supplies. They asked me who it was for and then they were not so enthusiastic to help. I could see this. Then they asked me if I was a member of their Church. I said no. And they said if I would become a member of their Church, they would give me some medicine."

"I can believe it," said Catherine, putting her head into her hands.

"Don't worry. I went to the U.S. Embassy and they gave me what I needed. I have some morphine," Tekeste explained. "Now you go home for awhile. I will stay with him and do what I can."

But for Dr. Jack Bronson help had come too late. Though he rested more comfortably with the medicine, his breathing was very labored. Just after Catherine returned to visit him that evening, JB squeezed her hand. "Thank you. I love you," and then he quietly died.

CHAPTER THIRTY-SIX

"Miss Catherine," the voice said.

"Yes."

"The Patriarch would like to speak to you. Could you hold the wire for a few minutes?"

"Yes, of course."

"Catherine my dear, how are you? I have been thinking and praying for you."

"I am fine. It is nice you call, Your Holiness."

"I just want to say we arranged a fine resting place for our Dr. Bronson. Because of his very special service to Ethiopia and the Church, we are giving him a very special resting place within our Church grounds."

Catherine knew that JB would have wanted to be buried in Ethiopia; his heart lay here among the Ethiopians he loved and had tried to help.

"Oh, Your Holiness," Catherine wept, "how kind of you. I know he would be so very, very pleased."

There was not one memorial service for Dr. Jack Bronson but five. The Mannesburg Mission, of course, out of a sense of duty, protocol and formality had a memorial service, one that Catherine found an ordeal.

They could not provide JB medicine, Catherine thought, but they could provide a service. The missionaries sat with expressionless faces and were totally helpless as to find any words of comfort.

The Evangelical Church also had scheduled a service, the rhetoric more sincere, but still Catherine could feel it was a matter of ritual. She was sure that for many they were glad to see JB gone and that with his passing, so too, was the whole topic of AIDS that so many found too difficult to accept.

It was the memorial service, however, of the young Ethiopians, the members of SAVE YOUR GENERATION, which brought tears to Catherine's eyes. It was lovely. There were poems, short essays, a drama act and songs.

Sitting outside under a clear blue sky with stark white clouds, the young people gathered and began by singing with much rhythm, deep drums beating in accompaniment:

Bronson, (drum beats)
Bronson (drum beats)
Bronson (drum beats)
Bronson (drum beats)

He loves others,
respects the work,
solution for the needy
his friends are proud of him

Let us praise him
Let us praise him

Let us remember his work

It was Bronson who fulfilled our needs
our association SYGA
always remember him
he was the beginner
and establisher
to love others
we learned from him
our Bronson's work
ever alive

Bronson (drum beats)
Bronson (drum beats)

He never complained of tiredness
always busy
to save human beings
was his motto
to save the generation
he was restless
we can't say Bronson has died
he replaced many of his followers
even though separated Bronson's alive
his spirit for work remains with us

Bronson (drum beats)
Bronson (drum beats)
Bronson (drum beats)

"We have lost a Crusader, our dear father, our leader,"
started Ato Solomon, "but Miss Catherine, we will always, always
remember him."
After the service, the young people invited everyone inside

for refreshment. On the wall was a picture of Jack Bronson with flowers hanging from its frame surrounded by seven candles. Underneath the picture was written, "Our dearest father, we will not forget you."

"For the next seven years, every July 22nd, we will have such a service for Dr. Bronson," Ato Solomon explained to Catherine.

Many weeks passed by before the shock of the past events began to make the first sign of easing.

"Have you heard what is going on at OSSA," Ato Solomon began to explain one day at coffee at Catherine's.

"I have heard bits and pieces," Catherine answered.

"Everyone is fighting for the power, for the position of Dr. Bronson. Even the young foreigners there are fighting for control."

"I am aware Solomon," Catherine responded sadly. "It is a difficult thing to witness what is going on. Sometimes humanity can be very disappointing. I really thought only these kinds of games happened in politics but the shock is they also happen in charity and aid work. It is hard for me to go through this chaos of OSSA as well."

"Why don't you come down and step in. You know what Dr. Bronson wanted to do. You knew him best."

"Because, Solomon, I don't have the strength to step into a struggle for power with these young foreigners there. I was already told by one young woman there, the only day I made a visit to OSSA, that I was certainly too old and too over qualified to step in to direct OSSA," Catherine tried to chuckle. "Can you imagine! All I would like to do is to keep Dr. Bronson's work going, but there are too many little scandals brewing about misuse of funds as well, Solomon."

"What will you do then, Catherine?"

"I am thinking that I would like to write about JB's work, about what I learned from him. I'd like to write that the sole object of the Christian Scriptures is charity and compassion and the characteristic of true compassion is that we take the trouble to get actually involved with the person or people concerned. This is what JB did. This is what he stood for and now I see how short the world is of such people."

"You know not one of us at SYGA believe anything that Dr. Vanden . . . Vande . . . what is his name said at Sodere. For the government it may just be a convenient excuse not to do any more work for AIDS. Why don't you think about staying with us and helping us to develop our organization?"

CHAPTER THIRTY-SEVEN

The weeks and months went by until two years had passed since the Sodere Conference. Catherine was busy with Save Your Generation. She designed workshops for them, educational programs and taught about AIDS and she had also finished writing her first novel based on the life of JB and his work in Ethiopia.

For Catherine, it was a chance to share JB's extraordinary life and philosophy which had so influenced her own life, that happiness is often found through a life dedicated to compassionate action. Her story stressed the need for the spirit of cooperation, sympathy and brotherhood and that a person could start anywhere, not necessarily in a poor country like Ethiopia, but anywhere in the world because the helpless and forgotten are in every country.

* * *

"I'm busy for the next two days," Catherine explained on the phone while signaling Solomon to sit. "I have a workshop for the Embassy Wives Club. They want to know everything about AIDS and possibly support some programs we have. I will call you when I have finished that program and we can schedule a workshop for your organization."

"Who was that?" Ato Solomon asked.

"It was the Netherlands Embassy. They would like to have a workshop just for their staff. I am getting so busy. My schedule is heavy. Word gets around especially when people hear that the government used to have about 60 AIDS staff workers at the Ministry of Health and now there are only 3. Of course, I explain that the government has decentralized their AIDS program but I do add that we have not seen the 57 remaining staff members employed in the various regions throughout Ethiopia. Sister Annemarie says doctors out in the rural areas estimate 55% of the sexually active population has HIV. These new trends catch the ears!"

"You will be asked to speak at more and more places," Solomon said. "That means you'll have to stay here forever and I like that."

"I think all I can do is help get the message across when I can, Solomon. International aid organizations can come and start water projects here, farming projects and educational programs; but what good is it if the AIDS pandemic is going to hit their target population the greatest."

"Miss Catherine, the phone again!"

"Hello."

"Catherine. It is Jackie at the Good Life Clinic."

"Hi! How are you?"

"I'm fine. I have something to tell you. But I think you should be sitting down."

"OK. What's up?"

"I just got a secret note from a laboratory worker in Aguna. I think you may have known him. He was a good friend of Dr. Bronson. His name is Ato Deresu."

"Oh for sure, the health assistant who also got training to be a laboratory specialist. What does he have to write that could be interesting?"

"You won't believe it. That is why I want you to sit down. It's highly secret and confidential. He writes it is only because he loved Dr. Bronson so much and is so sad at his loss that he has dared write me to tell you the news."

"Well, what is so important, Jackie. Do tell!"

"First, you must understand that if this were to get out, Deresu would lose his job forever."

"OK. Whatever it is I promise not to jeopardize his job by saying anything!"

"Your great friend Dr. Helmut Vandenbos has been sick for a number of months."

"What ever could make that guy sick I wonder?"

"You won't believe it. He is now so sick he is being flown out of Aguna tomorrow to Addis. Then, he is supposed to rest here a week and be flown to Europe."

"What is wrong with the great doctor anyway?"

"Deresu did blood samples. He had them confirmed. Your friend Dr. Helmut Vandenbos has AIDS."

About the Author

Patricia Ann Bluemel has a Ph.D. in Theocentric Psychology. In 1988, she left her home of Fort Lauderdale, Florida, a tourist's paradise, to accompany her husband to the deep bush of Ethiopia where he would work as a doctor at a mission hospital.

Confronted with the sharp contrast in lifestyle between the Developed and Less Developed Worlds, as well as encountering the challenging behavior of missionaries, Patricia fashions a story which in many ways is based on fact.

THE LOST CRUSADER highlights the nature of working in the medical field in Ethiopia, the obstacles of religious belief and practice, as well as the challenge in the fight against AIDS.

Now after the sudden death of her husband, Patricia has returned to Florida where she continues her work in the field of AIDS as the Executive Director of the Treasure Coast Community AIDS Network.